DATE DUE

A Background Note about
A Princess of Mars

A Princess of Mars was originally published in 1912. It was the first of a series of adventure books starring John Carter, a Civil War veteran, who unexpectedly finds himself relocated to the planet Mars. The book is often seen as an example of early science fiction, but it is perhaps better described as a truly fantastic adventure. As you will see, the red planet is anything but a dusty, barren place; it is a fantasy world complete with giant green barbarians and a beautiful maiden in distress. You are about to participate in an otherworldly, epic story that has proved to be such a wonderful entertainment that it endures to this very day.

EDGAR RICE BURROUGHS

A PRINCESS OF MARS

Edited by Denton Cairnes
Afterword by Beth Johnson

 THE TOWNSEND LIBRARY

A PRINCESS OF MARS

TP **THE TOWNSEND LIBRARY**

For more titles in the Townsend Library,
visit our website: **www.townsendpress.com**

Townsend Press, Inc.
439 Kelley Drive
West Berlin, New Jersey 08091
cs@townsendpress.com

ISBN-13: 978-1-59194-061-6
ISBN-10: 1-59194-061-3

Library of Congress Control Number:
2005936425

Contents

CHAPTER 1

On the Arizona Hills

I am a very old man. I am a hundred years old, maybe more, but I have never aged like other men. As far as I can recall, I have always been a man of about thirty. I look the same as I did forty years ago, and yet I feel that I cannot go on living forever—that some day I will die the real death from which there is no return.

Because of this, I have decided to write down the interesting periods of my life. I cannot explain these happenings. I can only describe in the words of an ordinary soldier of fortune the strange events that happened to me during the ten years that my dead body lay in an Arizona cave.

I have never told this story before, and no one will see this manuscript until after I have passed on. I have no desire to be ridiculed by the public, the pulpit, and the press—held up as a liar—when I am only telling the simple truths which some day science will confirm.

My name is John Carter but I am better known as Captain John Carter of Virginia. At the close of the Civil War I found myself with several thousand dollars in worthless Confederate money and the rank of captain in an army that no longer existed. I was a servant of the Confederate States of America, which had vanished along with the hopes of the South. Masterless, penniless, and with my only means of livelihood gone, I decided to work my way to the southwest and search for gold.

I spent a year prospecting in the company of Captain James K. Powell of Richmond. We were extremely fortunate and located a remarkable gold-bearing quartz vein, more valuable than anything in our wildest dreams. We decided that one of us must return to civilization and return with a crew of men and equipment to properly work the mine.

Powell was familiar with the country, so we decided that he should make the trip. I would stay behind and protect our site from any claim-jumpers. On March 3, 1866, Powell mounted his horse and led two loaded burros down the mountainside on the first stage of his journey.

The morning was clear and beautiful and I could see him and his pack animals plodding their way toward the valley. For most of the day I would catch glimpses of them as they topped a ridge or came out on a level plateau. My last sight of Powell was about three in the afternoon as he entered the shadows on the far side of the valley.

Some half hour later I happened to glance across the valley and was surprised to see three little dots in about the same place I had last seen my friend and his pack animals. I am not given to needless worrying, but the more I tried to convince myself that all was well with Powell and that the dots I had seen were antelope, the less I was able to assure myself.

Since we had entered the territory we had not seen a single hostile Indian. We had been told of the great numbers of these vicious raiders who were supposed to haunt the trails, murdering any white man who fell in to their merciless clutches.

I knew Powell was a well-armed, experienced Indian fighter, but I also knew that his chances were small against a party of Apaches. Finally, I could no longer endure the suspense, and arming myself with my two Colt revolvers and a carbine, I strapped on two belts of cartridges, mounted my saddle horse, and started off down Powell's trail.

As soon as I reached level ground I urged my mount into a slow run and continued until I discovered the point where other tracks joined Powell's. They were the tracks of three unshod ponies—INDIANS!

I followed at a faster pace until darkness set in and I was forced to wait for the rising moon. As I waited, I had time to think about the wisdom of my chase. I pondered the possibility that I had imagined the dangers. When I caught up with Powell we would both get a good laugh for my pains.

By nine o'clock the moon was bright enough for me to proceed, and about midnight I reached the water hole where Powell had expected to camp. I found the spot deserted, but I saw that the tracks of the pursuing horsemen continued after Powell with only a brief stop for water.

I was now positive that the three riders trailing him were Apaches and they wished to capture Powell alive for what evil purposes I could only imagine. I urged my horse onward, hoping that I would catch up with the Indians before they attacked him.

Further speculation was cut short by the faint sound of two shots far ahead. I knew that Powell would need me now, and I urged my horse up the narrow mountain trail. I had forged ahead a mile or so when the trail suddenly opened onto a small level field. The sight that met my eyes filled me with dread and dismay.

The stretch of level land was white with Indian tepees, and there were probably half a thousand warriors clustered around some object near the center of the camp. Their attention was riveted to this point of interest. I could have turned back into the dark and made my escape with perfect safety.

I do not believe that I am made of heroic stuff, because in all of the hundreds of acts that have placed me face to face with death, I cannot recall a single one where any alternative occurred to me until hours later. My mind is such that I am subconsciously forced into the path of duty without even thinking about it.

I was positive that Powell was the center of attraction, and the instant I viewed the scene I whipped out my revolvers and was charging down on the entire army of warriors, shooting rapidly, and whooping at the top of my lungs. I could not have chosen better tactics, for the red men, surprised and convinced that a troop of cavalry was attacking, turned and fled in every direction for their rifles and bows and arrows.

The view after the crowd's panic-stricken flight filled me with rage. Under the clear rays of the Arizona moon lay Powell, his body bristling with arrows. Riding up close to him. I reached down, grabbed his cartridge belt and drew him up across my saddle. A backward glance convinced me that to return by the way I had come would be more hazardous than to continue forward, so putting spurs to my poor beast, I made a dash for the far side.

The Indians discovered that I was alone, and I was pursued with curses, threats, arrows, and bullets! The facts that it is difficult to aim anything but curses and threats accurately by moonlight; that they were upset by the unexpected manner of my arrival; and that I was a rapidly moving target; saved me from their various deadly projectiles and permitted me to reach the shadows of the surrounding peaks.

My horse was traveling practically unguided, and so it happened that he entered a shallow gully that led to the summit of the range and not to the pass that I had hoped would carry me to safety. However, I owe my life and my remarkable adventures to this turn in the road.

My first hint that I was on the wrong trail came when I heard the yells of the pursuing savages suddenly grow fainter. I stopped on a ledge overlooking the trail and saw them disappearing around the bend. I knew they would quickly discover they were on the wrong trail and the search for me would be renewed as soon as they located my tracks.

I went just a short distance farther when an excellent trail opened up. The trail was level and broad and led upward and in the general direction I wished to go. The cliff rose for several hundred feet on my right, and on my left was an equal drop to the bottom of a rocky ravine. I followed this trail for a hundred yards when a sharp turn to the right brought me to the mouth of a cave. It was now morning, and daylight came almost without warning.

Dismounting, I laid Powell on the ground and my most painstaking examination failed to reveal any spark of life. I forced water from my canteen between his dead lips, bathed his face and rubbed his hands, working over him continuously for the better part of an hour until I had to face the fact that he was dead.

I was very fond of Powell, a polished southern gentleman and a loyal and true friend. It was with deepest grief that I finally gave up my crude attempt to revive him. I left him on the ledge and then crept into the cave to check it out. I found a large chamber, with a smooth and well-worn floor. The back of the cave was so lost in dense shadow that I could not see if there were openings into other chambers.

As I was examining the cave, I started to feel a pleasant drowsiness creeping over me that I blamed on the fatigue of my long and strenuous ride and the excitement of the fight and pursuit. I felt comparatively safe in my present location, since I knew that one man could defend the trail to the cave against an army.

I soon became so drowsy that I could barely resist the strong desire to throw myself on the ground for a few moments' rest. I knew that this would never do, as it would mean certain death at the hands of my red friends, who might be upon me at any moment. With an effort I started back toward the opening of the cave only to stumble drunkenly and slide down to the floor.

CHAPTER 2

The Escape of the Dead

A sense of delicious dreaminess came over me, my muscles relaxed, and I was at the point of giving way to my desire to sleep when the sound of approaching horses reached my ears. I tried to spring to my feet but was horrified to discover that my muscles refused to respond! I was now thoroughly awake, but unable to move. It was as though I had turned to stone. Then, for the first time, I noticed a slight vapor and a faintly pungent odor filling the cave, and I thought I had been overcome by some poisonous gas. I could not understand why I kept my mental faculties but was not able to move.

I was on the cave floor facing the opening from where I could see the short stretch of trail between the cave and the turn of the cliff. The noise of the approaching horses stopped, and I judged the Indians were creeping up along the ledge to my living tomb. I did not wait long before a sound warned me of their nearness, and then a face, streaked with war-paint, edged around the shoulder of the cliff, and savage eyes looked directly into mine. I was sure that he could see me because the early morning sun was shining through the cave's opening.

The warrior, instead of approaching, merely stood and stared—his eyes bulged and his jaw dropped. And then another savage face appeared, and a third and fourth and fifth. Each face was the picture of awe and fear, but for what reason I did not know, nor did I learn about it until ten years later.

Suddenly a low moaning sound came from the back of the cave, and as it reached the ears of the Indians, they turned and fled in panic-stricken terror. So frantic were their efforts to escape that one of the braves was shoved, screaming, off the cliff to the rocks below. The rest of the band's wild cries echoed in the canyon for a short time, and then all was still once more.

The sound that frightened them was not repeated, but it was enough to start me speculating on the unknown horror that lurked in the shadows at my back. I was paralyzed—with my back to some horrible danger whose very sound caused the ferocious Apache warriors to turn in wild stampede. They fled like a flock of sheep would run from a pack of wolves. This was a fearsome predicament, especially for a physically powerful man like me who had always fought with all his energy.

Several times I thought I heard faint sounds behind me like someone moving cautiously, but eventually even these ceased, and I was left helplessly to think about my situation. My paralysis was a mystery to me, and my only hope was that it might go away as suddenly as it had come.

Late in the afternoon, my horse started slowly down the trail in search of food and water. I was left alone with the unknown entity in the back of the cave and the dead body of my friend, which lay just within my range of vision.

From then until midnight all was silence—the silence of the dead. Then, the awful moaning started up again. I heard the sound in the back shadows, and also a faint rustling like dead leaves. The shock to my already overstrained nervous system was terrible, and with superhuman effort I tried to break my awful bonds. It was an effort of the mind, will, and nerves—not muscular, for I could not move so much as my little finger, though I tried with all my might. And then something gave and I found myself standing with my back against the wall of the cave facing my unknown foe.

Moonlight flooded the cave and there before me lay my own body as it had been lying all these hours, with the eyes staring toward the cave's opening and the hands resting limply on the ground. In utter confusion I looked first at my lifeless form on the floor, and then down at myself against the wall—for there I lay clothed, and yet here I stood naked as at the moment of birth.

The transition had been so sudden and so unexpected that, for a moment, it left me forgetful of anything other than my strange transformation. My first thought was, is this death? Have I passed over into that other life? But I could not believe this, since I could feel my heart pounding against my ribs from my efforts to release myself from the ailment that possessed me. My breath was coming in quick, short gasps, and cold sweat stood out from every pore of my body, so I knew that I was something other than a ghost.

Again I was suddenly made aware of my immediate surroundings by a repetition of the weird moan from the depths of the cave. Naked and unarmed as I was, I had no desire to face the unseen thing menacing me.

My revolvers were in their holsters on my lifeless body and, for some reason, I could not bring myself to go near them. My carbine was strapped to my saddle, and as my horse had wandered off, I was left without any means of defense. My only alternative was to flee, and my decision was helped by a recurrence of the rustling sound from the thing that now seemed to be creeping up on me.

Unable to resist the temptation to escape this horrible place, I jumped quickly through the opening into the starlight of a clear Arizona night. The crisp, fresh mountain air outside the cave acted as an immediate tonic and I felt new life and new courage coursing through me. I reasoned that I had been helpless in the cave for many hours, yet nothing had harmed me, and my better judgment convinced me that the noises I had heard resulted from purely natural and harmless causes.

I decided to investigate, but first I lifted my head to fill my lungs with the pure, invigorating night air of the mountains. As I did so, I saw stretching far below me the beautiful vista of a rocky gorge merging into a level plain covered with cactus, changed by the moonlight into a miracle of soft splendor and wondrous enchantment.

Few wonders are more inspiring than the beauties of an Arizona moonlit landscape. The silvered mountains in the distance, the strange lights and shadows on ridge and gully, and the grotesque details of the stiff, yet beautiful cactus form a picture both enchanting and inspiring. It's like one were catching a glimpse of some dead and forgotten world, different from any other spot on Earth.

As I stood meditating, I turned my gaze to the heavens where the thousands of stars formed a gorgeous canopy for the wonders of the earthly scene. A large red star, close to the distant horizon, riveted my attention. As I gazed, I felt a spell of overpowering fascination—it was Mars, the red planet, named for the god of war, and for me, the fighting man, it had always held the power of enchantment. As I gazed at it on that night, it seemed to call me, to lure me, to draw me like a magnet attracts a particle of iron.

My longing was beyond the power of opposition; I closed my eyes, stretched out my arms, and felt myself drawn through the boundless vastness of space. There was an instant of extreme cold and then . . . utter darkness.

My Advent on Mars

I opened my eyes to a strange and remarkable landscape. My inner consciousness told me that I was on Mars as plainly as your conscious mind tells you that you are on Earth. You do not question the fact and neither did I.

I found myself lying on a bed of yellowish, moss-like vegetation that stretched around me in all directions for miles. I seemed to be lying in a deep, circular basin and along one outer edge I could see some low hills.

It was midday, the sun was shining on me and the heat was rather intense on my naked body, but no more than under similar conditions in an Arizona desert. A little to my left, perhaps a hundred yards away, I saw a low, walled enclosure about four feet in height. No water and no vegetation other than the moss was in sight, and as I was somewhat thirsty, I decided to do a little exploring.

Springing to my feet I received my first Martian surprise, for the effort, which on Earth would have brought me standing upright, carried me into the Martian air twelve feet off the ground! I landed softly without any appreciable shock.

My muscles, perfectly accustomed to the force of gravity on Earth, played mischief with the lesser gravitation and lower air pressure on Mars. I found that I had to learn to walk all over again, as the muscular exertion used easily and safely on Earth played strange antics with me on this planet. My attempts to walk resulted in a variety of hops which took me a couple of feet off the ground with each step and ended up with me sprawling on my face.

However, I was determined to explore the strange structure—the only evidence of habitation in sight—and in a few moments had reached its low, encircling wall. There appeared to be no doors or windows on the side nearest me, but as the wall was only four feet high, I cautiously got to my feet and peered over the top at the strangest sight I had ever seen.

The roof of the enclosure was of solid glass about four inches thick, and under it were several hundred large eggs, perfectly round and snowy white, about two feet in diameter. Five or six had already hatched and the freakish creatures blinking in the sunlight were enough to cause me to doubt my sanity. They seemed mostly head, with little scrawny bodies, long necks and six legs, or, as I later learned, two legs and two arms, with a middle pair of limbs which could be used as either arms or legs. Their eyes were set at the sides of their heads and protruded in such a manner that they could be directed either forward or back and also independently of each other, permitting this strange animal to look in any direction, or in two directions at once, without needing to turn its head.

The ears, slightly above the eyes and closer together, were small and cup-shaped, protruding up about an inch. Their noses were mere slits in the center of their faces, midway between their mouths and ears.

There was no hair on their light yellowish-green colored bodies. In the adults, as I was to learn quite soon, this color deepens to an olive green and is darker in the male than in the female. Further, the heads of the adults are not so out of proportion to their bodies as in the case of the young.

The iris of the eyes is blood red, while the pupil is dark. The eyeball itself is very white, as are the teeth. These latter add a most ferocious look to an already fearsome appearance, as the lower tusks curve upward to sharp points that end about where the eyes of earthly human beings are located. Against the dark background of their green skin, their white tusks stand out in a most striking manner, making them appear to be fearsome weapons.

Most of these details I noted later, for I had little time to speculate on the wonders of my new discovery. I had seen that the eggs were in the process of hatching, and as I stood watching the hideous little monsters break from their shells I failed to note the approach of a group of full-grown Martians.

Coming, as they did, over the soft and soundless moss, which covers practically the entire surface of Mars with the exception of the frozen areas at the poles and the scattered culti-vated districts, they might have captured me eas-ily, but that was not their intention. It was the rattling of the lead warrior's weapons that warned me.

I often marvel that my life hung on such a lit-tle thing and that I escaped death so easily. If the leader's rifle had not rattled against his spear, I would have been snuffed out without even know-ing that death was near. But that small sound caused me to turn, and there, not ten feet from my chest, was the fast approaching point of a huge spear, tipped with gleaming metal! This dreadful weapon was held at the side of a mounted replica of the little devils I had just been watching.

But how puny and harmless the hatchlings now looked beside this huge and horrible picture of hate, vengeance, and death! The creature himself was at least fifteen feet in height and, on Earth, would have weighed some four hundred pounds. He rode his mount as we ride a horse, grasping the animal's sides with his lower limbs, while the hands of his two right arms held his spear. The animal he rode had neither bridle nor reins for guidance.

And his mount! How can earthly words describe it? It towered ten feet at the shoulder and had four legs on either side. Its broad flat tail, larger at the tip than at the root, was held straight out behind. It had a gaping, tooth filled mouth that split its head from its snout to its long, massive neck.

Like its master, it was entirely devoid of hair, but was a smooth and glossy dark slate color. Its belly was white, and its legs shaded from the slate of its shoulders and hips to a vivid yellow at the feet. The feet themselves were heavily padded, which contributed to the noiselessness of their approach. Padded feet and multiple legs are common features of the animals of Mars.

Behind this first charging demon trailed the others, similar in all respects, but as I learned later, bearing individual characteristics. This picture, or rather nightmare, which I have described at length, made but one terrible and swift impression on me as I turned to meet it.

Unarmed and naked as I was, the first law of nature demanded that the only possible solution to my immediate problem was to get away from the point of that charging spear. I attempted a leap up to the top of the Martian egg incubator. My effort surprised both me and the Martian warriors. It carried me at least thirty feet into the air and landed me a hundred feet from my pursuers on the opposite side of the enclosure.

I landed on the soft moss easily and turned and saw my enemies lined up along the far wall. Some were surveying me with astonishment, and the others were satisfying themselves that I had not disturbed their young hatchlings. They were conversing in low tones and pointing toward me. Their discovery that I had not harmed the little Martians, and that I was unarmed, must have caused them to look on me with less hostility. As I was to learn later, the thing that weighed most in my favor was my exhibition of jumping.

While the Martians are immense, their bones are very large and they are muscled only in proportion to the gravity that they must overcome. The result is that they are infinitely less agile and powerful, in proportion to their weight, than an Earth man. My feat was as marvelous on Mars as it would have been on Earth, and instead of wanting to kill me, they suddenly looked at me as a wonderful discovery to be captured and exhibited back at their camp.

The break my unexpected agility provided allowed me time to think about my immediate future. I was also able to note more closely the appearance of the warriors and saw that each was armed with several other weapons in addition to a spear. Every one of them was equipped with a rifle, and that was the weapon that caused me to reconsider my thoughts of escape. I felt, for some reason, they were particularly efficient in handling this weapon.

These rifles were of a white metal with a stock of wood. With the rifle's small caliber, explosive, radium bullets, and the long length of the barrel, they are deadly at ranges which would be unthinkable on Earth. The theoretical range of this rifle is three miles, but the best they can do in actual service when equipped with their wireless finders and sights is a little over one mile. My later knowledge was enough to give me great respect for the Martian firearm, and some mysterious force must have warned me against an attempt to escape in broad daylight from under the muzzles of so many of these death-dealing machines.

The Martians, after conversing for a short time, turned and rode away in the direction from which they had come, leaving one of their number by the enclosure. They halted at about two hundred yards, and turning their mounts, sat watching the two of us.

He was evidently the leader of the band. I noted that the rest of the group seemed to have moved to their present position at his direction. When he saw that his band of warriors had come to a halt, he dismounted, threw down his spear and small arms, and came around the end of the incubator toward me, entirely unarmed except for the ornaments strapped to his head, limbs, and chest.

As he approached, he unclasped a metal armlet, and holding it toward me in the open palm of his hand, addressed me in a clear, resonant voice, but in a language, it is needless to say, I could not understand. He then stopped as though waiting for my reply, aiming his ears and turning his strange-looking eyes toward me.

As the silence became painful I decided to hazard a little conversation of my own. The throwing down of his weapons and the withdrawing of his troop before his advance toward me would have signified a peaceful mission anywhere on Earth, so why not on Mars?

Placing my hand over my heart, I explained to him that while I did not understand his language, his actions spoke for the peace and friendship that at the present moment were most dear to my heart. Of course, I might have been a babbling brook for all the meaning my speech carried to him, but he understood my action.

Stretching my hand toward him, I advanced and took the armlet from his open palm, clasping it around my arm above the elbow. I then smiled at him and stood waiting. His wide mouth spread into an answering smile, and locking one of his intermediary arms in mine we turned and walked back toward his mount. At the same time he motioned his followers to advance. They started toward us in a wild run, but were checked by a signal from him. He probably feared that if I were to be frightened again I might jump entirely out of the landscape.

He exchanged a few words with his men, motioned to me that I would ride behind one of them, and then mounted his own animal. The fellow designated reached down two hands and lifted me up behind him on the glossy back of his mount, where I hung on as best I could by the belts and straps that held the Martian's weapons and ornaments. The entire troop then turned and galloped away toward the range of hills in the distance.

CHAPTER 4

A Prisoner

We had gone perhaps ten miles when the ground began to rise and after crossing a narrow gorge we came to an open valley. At the valley's far end was a low plain where I saw an enormous city. We entered it by what appeared to be a ruined roadway leading out from the immense urban buildup.

I saw that the buildings were deserted, and while not greatly decayed, had the appearance of not having been inhabited for years. We entered a large plaza and I saw here and in the surrounding buildings almost a thousand of the green creatures.

With the exception of their ornaments and some sort of leather harness, all were naked. The women varied in appearance just a little from the men. The men's tusks were much larger in proportion to their height. The women's bodies were smaller and lighter in color. The adult females ranged in height from ten to twelve feet. The children were even lighter green in color than the women, and all looked alike except that some were older and taller than others.

I saw no signs of extreme age among them, nor was there any noticeable difference in their appearance from the age of maturity, about forty, to around one thousand years of age. At that advanced age, they go voluntarily on their last strange pilgrimage down the River Iss. No living Martian knows where this river goes and no Martian has ever returned from this last trip.

Only about one Martian in a thousand dies of sickness or disease, and possibly twenty take the voluntary trip down the River Iss. Many of the others die violent deaths in duels, hunting, accidents, and war. But the greatest death loss of this species comes during the age of childhood, when vast numbers of the little Martians fall victims to the great white apes.

The average life expectancy of a Martian after the age of maturity is about three hundred years, but would be nearer one thousand if it were not for the various means leading to violent death. Owing to the waning resources of the planet it became necessary to counteract the increasing life span produced by their remarkable medical skill. So life is considered lightly on Mars, as is evidenced by their dangerous sports and the almost continual warfare between the various communities. There are other causes weeding out the population, but nothing contributes as much as the fact that no Martian is ever voluntarily without a weapon.

As we neared the plaza and my presence was noticed, we were surrounded by hundreds of the creatures. Some of them seemed to want to pluck me from my guard's riding beast but a word from the leader stilled their clamor, and we proceeded across the plaza to the entrance of a beautiful structure.

The building was low, but covered an enormous area. It was constructed of gleaming white marble inlaid with gold and brilliant stones. Our party halted at the entrance and I was lowered to the ground. Again the leader locked his arm in mine and we proceeded into the audience chamber.

On the floor of this large room, which was dotted with highly carved wooden desks and chairs, were about forty male Martians. On an elevated platform squatted an enormous warrior heavily loaded with metal ornaments, colored feathers and beautifully worked leather trappings set with precious stones. A short cape of white fur lined with brilliant scarlet silk hung from his shoulders.

There were few formalities observed in

approaching the Martian chieftain. My captor merely strode up to the rostrum. The chieftain rose to his feet and uttered the name of my escort who, in turn, halted and repeated the name of the ruler followed by his title.

At the time, this ceremony and the words they uttered meant nothing to me, but later I learned that this was the customary greeting between green Martians. Had the two been strangers, and therefore unable to exchange names, they would have silently exchanged ornaments if their mission had been peaceful—otherwise they would have exchanged shots or fought out their introduction with some other weapons.

What struck me most about this assemblage and the hall was that the creatures were out of proportion to the desks, chairs, and other furnishings. The furniture was sized for human beings such as I, and the great bulks of the Martians could barely squeeze into the chairs. Evidently there were inhabitants of Mars other than these wild and grotesque creatures. But the evidence of antiquity all around me indicated that these buildings belonged to some long-extinct race.

My captor, whose name was Tars Tarkas, was the vice-chieftain of the community and a great statesman and warrior. He briefly explained the incidents connected with his expedition, including my capture, and, when he had concluded, the chieftain addressed me.

I replied in English merely to convince him that neither of us could understand the other. But I noticed that when I smiled slightly on concluding, he did likewise. This fact, and the similar occurrence during my first talk with Tars Tarkas, convinced me that we had at least something in common—the ability to smile, therefore to laugh; denoting a sense of humor. But I was to learn that the Martian smile is superficial, and that the Martian laugh is a thing to cause strong men to blanch in horror.

The assembled warriors examined me closely, feeling my muscles and the texture of my skin. The principal chieftain then signified a desire to see me perform, and motioning me to follow, he walked to the open plaza.

I had made no attempt to walk since my first failure, except while holding on to my captor's arm. I now went skipping among the desks and chairs like some monstrous grasshopper and having a very difficult time. After bruising myself severely, much to the amusement of the Martians, I again tried crawling, but this did not suit them and I was roughly jerked to my feet by one of the laughing giant creatures.

As he banged me down on my feet I did the only thing a gentleman might do under these circumstances of brutality, boorishness, and lack of consideration for a stranger's rights—I swung my fist squarely into his jaw and he went down like a felled ox. As he dropped to the floor I wheeled around with my back toward the nearest desk, expecting to be overwhelmed by the vengeance of his comrades.

My fears were groundless, however, as the other Martians, at first struck dumb with wonderment, finally broke into wild peals of laughter and applause. I did not recognize the applause as such, but later, when I had become acquainted with their customs, I learned that I had won what they seldom granted, a display of approval.

The fellow I struck lay where he had fallen and none of his mates approached him. Tars Tarkas advanced toward me, holding out one of his arms, and we then proceeded to the plaza without further mishap. I did not, of course, know the reason we had come to the open space, but it was not long before I figured it out. They first repeated the word "sak" a number of times, and then Tars Tarkas made several jumps, repeating the same word before each leap. He then turned to me and said, "sak!" I saw what they were after, and gathering myself, I "sakked" with such marvelous success that I cleared a good hundred and fifty feet and landed squarely on my feet without falling. I then returned by easy jumps of about thirty feet to the little group of warriors.

My exhibition was witnessed by several hundred of the lesser Martians, and they immediately broke into demands for a repetition, which the chieftain ordered me to perform. But I was both hungry and thirsty, and decided that my only method of relief was to demand some consideration from these creatures. I ignored the repeated commands to "sak," and each time they were made I motioned to my mouth and rubbed my stomach.

Tars Tarkas and the chief exchanged a few words and then Tars Tarkas called to a young female among the throng, gave her some instructions and motioned for me to go along with her. I grasped her arm and together we crossed the plaza toward a large building on the far side.

My fair companion was about eight feet tall, having just arrived at maturity, but not yet to her full height. She was of a light olive-green color, with a smooth, glossy hide. Her name, as I learned afterward, was Sola, and she was one of Tars Tarkas's many attendants. She led me to a spacious chamber in one of the buildings fronting the plaza.

The room was bright from a number of large windows and was beautifully decorated with mural paintings and other art works. But the aura of antiquity over the space convinced me that the builders of these wonderful creations had nothing in common with the crude half-brutes now present.

Sola motioned me to be seated on a pile of silks near the center of the room and she then turned and made a peculiar hissing sound, as though signaling to someone. In response to her call I got my first sight of a new Martian wonder. It waddled in on its ten short legs, and squatted down in front of the girl like an obedient puppy. The thing was the size of a Shetland pony, but its head bore a slight resemblance to a frog, except that the jaws were equipped with three rows of long, sharp tusks.

CHAPTER 5

I Elude My Watch Dog

Sola stared into the brute's wicked-looking eyes, muttered a command, pointed to me, and left the chamber. I could only wonder what this strange monster might do when left alone in the room with me. But I saw my fears were groundless as I watched the beast cross the room to the only exit and lay down across the threshold. This was my first experience with a Martian calot, but it was not to be my last, for this beast guarded me during the entire time I was a captive among these green men. Twice he saved my life, and he was never voluntarily away from me.

While Sola was away, I examined the room. The murals depicted scenes of wonderful beauty—mountains, rivers, lakes, oceans, meadows, trees and flowers, winding roadways, sun-kissed gardens—scenes which might have portrayed earthly views but for the different colorings of the vegetation. The work had been done by master artists, so subtle the atmosphere, so perfect the technique. But there was no illustration of an animal or human so I could see what these other inhabitants of Mars looked like.

While I was thinking about the strange things I had thus far seen on Mars, Sola returned with food and drink. The food consisted of some solid substance, the consistency of cheese, while the liquid was apparently milk from some animal. It was not unpleasant to the taste and I learned in a short time to prize it highly. I later discovered it came from a large plant.

After I had eaten, I stretched out on the silks and was soon asleep. I must have slept several hours—it was dark when I awoke—and I was very cold. I noticed that someone had thrown a fur over me, but it had become dislodged and in the darkness I could not see to replace it. Suddenly a hand reached out and pulled the fur over me, shortly afterward adding another to my covering.

My watchful guardian was Sola. This girl, alone of all the green Martians, showed characteristics of sympathy, kindness, and affection. Her attention to me was constant and unfailing, and her care saved me from many hardships.

As I was to learn, the Martian nights are extremely cold. The nights are either brilliantly illuminated or very dark, for if neither of the two moons of Mars happens to be in the sky almost total darkness results, since the very thin atmosphere fails to diffuse starlight. On the other hand, if both moons are in the heavens the night is very bright.

The nearer moon of Mars makes a revolution around the planet in about seven hours. She may be seen hurtling through the sky a couple of times each night, revealing all her phases during each path across the night sky. The farther moon revolves around Mars every thirty hours, and together with her sister satellite makes a night-time Martian scene one of weird grandeur.

After Sola had rearranged my coverings I went back to sleep and did not wake up again until daylight. The watchdog was still stretched across the threshold. He had not moved a muscle, his eyes were still glued on me, and I wondered what might happen if I tried to escape. I have always been prone to seek adventure and investigate where wiser men would have left well enough alone. It now occurred to me that the surest way of learning the attitude of this beast would be to attempt to leave the room. I felt sure I could escape him once I was outside the building for I could see from the shortness of his legs that the brute was no jumper and probably no runner.

Slowly I gained my feet and advanced toward

him. As I neared the brute he backed away from me, and when I reached the doorway he moved to one side to let me pass. He then fell in behind me and followed as I made my way along the deserted street.

Evidently his mission was only to protect me, but when we reached the edge of the city he got in front of me, uttering strange sounds and baring his ferocious tusks. Thinking to have some amusement at his expense, I rushed toward him, and when almost on him jumped into the air, landing far beyond him and away from the city. He wheeled and charged me with the most appalling speed I had ever seen! I had thought his short legs would hinder his swiftness, but if he had been running with greyhounds they would have looked like they were asleep. As I was to learn, the calot is the fleetest animal on Mars, and owing to its intelligence, loyalty, and ferocity, is used in hunting, war, and as the protector of the green Martian man.

I saw that I would have difficulty in escaping his fangs on a straight course so I met his charge by doubling back on my tracks and leaping over him just as he was almost on me. This trick gave me a considerable advantage, and I was able to reach the city ahead of him, and as he came tearing after me I jumped up to a second story window in one of the buildings.

I pulled myself up and gazed down at the

baffled animal. My victory was short-lived, however, for hardly had I gained a secure seat when a
huge hand grabbed me from behind! I was pulled
inside and thrown on my back and saw standing
over me a colossal ape-like creature, white and
hairless except for an enormous shock of bristly
hair on its head.

A Fight that Won Friends

The creature, which resembled our earthly men more than it did the green Martians, held me to the ground with one huge foot, while it jabbered at another creature behind me. This other ape soon came toward us, swinging a stone club.

The creatures were about ten feet tall, and had, like the green Martians, an extra set of arms or legs, midway between their upper and lower limbs. Their eyes were set close together and non-protruding. Their ears were placed high while their snouts and teeth seemed like those of our African gorilla. Altogether they did not look so bad when viewed in comparison to the green Martians.

The club was swinging toward my face when suddenly a bolt of multi-legged horror hurled itself through the doorway and onto my executioner!

With a shriek of fear, the ape holding me jumped through the open window. But its companion fought in a terrible struggle with my rescuer, which was nothing less than my faithful calot watch-thing.

I got to my feet and edged back as I witnessed a battle like no human had ever seen. The strength, agility, and blind ferocity of these two creatures was amazing. My beast had an advantage in his first hold, having sunk his fangs into the chest of his adversary. But the strong arms and big hands of the ape, backed by muscles far larger than those of the Martian men I had seen, had locked on the throat of my guardian. The ape was slowly choking out his life.

They rolled back and forth, neither one emitting a sound of fear or pain. I saw the eyes of my beast bulging from their sockets and blood flowing from its nostrils. It was clear that he was getting weaker, but so was the ape, whose struggles were growing less violent. Suddenly I came to my senses and seized the fallen club! Swinging it with all the power of my earthly arms, I struck the head of the ape, crushing it like an eggshell.

Scarcely had the blow descended when I was faced with a new danger. The ape's partner, recovered from its first shock of terror, had returned. I was filled with fear as I watched him coming through the doorway, raging and frothing at the mouth.

I am always willing to stand and fight when the odds are not too much against me, but in this instance I saw neither glory nor profit in pitting my relatively puny strength against the iron muscles of this enraged creature of an unknown world. In fact, there could be only one outcome from such an encounter as far as I was concerned.

I was standing near the window and I knew that once in the street I might reach the safety of the plaza before the creature could overtake me. At least there was a chance for safety in flight, against almost certain death if I should remain and fight. It is true I held the club, but what could I do with it against his four large arms? Even if I could break one with my first blow he could reach out and get me with the others before I could recover.

As these thoughts passed through my mind my eyes stopped on my injured guardian lying on the floor. He lay gasping, his eyes locked on me in what seemed an appeal for protection. I could not ignore that look, nor could I desert my rescuer without giving as good an account of myself on his behalf as he had on mine.

I turned to meet the charge of the crazed bull ape. He was now too close to me for the club, so I just threw it at him. It struck just below his knees, generating a howl of pain and rage, and throwing him off balance. He lunged at me with his arms stretched wide.

Again, as on the preceding day, I used my earthly fighting tactics, and swung my right fist to the point of his chin and followed with a left to his stomach. The effect was marvelous—as I lightly sidestepped after delivering the second blow, he reeled and fell on the floor gasping for wind. Leaping over his body, I seized the club and finished off the monster.

As I delivered the final blow a laugh rang out. I turned and saw Tars Tarkas, Sola, and three warriors standing in the doorway. I was, for the second time, the recipient of their zealously guarded applause. My absence had been discovered by Sola and she quickly informed Tars Tarkas, who set out immediately to search for me. As they had approached the city limits they saw the bull ape as he bolted into the building, wild with rage.

They followed immediately behind him and had witnessed my short but decisive battle. This encounter, together with my fight on the previous day and my feats of jumping, placed me high in their regard. Not having feelings of friendship, love, or affection, these people just about worship physical prowess and bravery, and nothing is too good for the object of their adoration as long as he maintains his position by repeated examples of his skill, strength, and courage.

Sola was the only one of the Martians whose face had not been twisted in laughter as I battled for my life. She was very concerned and, as soon as I had finished off the monster, rushed to me and carefully examined my body for possible injuries. Satisfying herself that I had come out of the fight with no wounds, she smiled quietly, and taking my hand, started toward the door of the chamber.

Tars Tarkas and the other warriors were standing over the brute which had saved my life, and whose life I, in turn, had saved. They seemed to be deep in argument, and finally one of them addressed me, but remembering my ignorance of his language turned back to Tars Tarkas, who, with a word and gesture, gave some command and turned to follow us from the room.

I sensed something threatening in their attitude toward my beast, and I hesitated to leave until I learned the outcome. It was well I did, for the warrior drew a pistol and was aiming at the creature when I sprang forward and struck his arm just as he fired. The bullet hit the wall and exploded, blowing a hole completely through the wood and masonry.

I then knelt down beside the wounded, though still fearsome, animal and raising it to its feet, motioned for it to follow me. The Martians were astounded—they could not understand attitudes such as gratitude and compassion. The warrior with the gun looked at Tars Tarkas, but the latter signaled that I be left to my own devices, and so we returned to the plaza with my beast following at my heels, and Sola grasping me tightly by the arm.

I now had at least two friends on Mars—a young woman who watched over me with motherly attention, and a dumb brute which held in its ugly carcass more love, loyalty, and gratitude than could have been found in the entire five million green Martians who wandered the deserted cities and dead seas of Mars.

Child-Raising on Mars

After a breakfast, which was a repeat of the meal of the preceding day and duplicated in practically every meal that followed while I was with the green men of Mars, Sola escorted me to the plaza. Here I found the entire community engaged in watching or helping at the harnessing of huge mastodon-like animals to large three-wheeled chariots. There were about two hundred and fifty of these vehicles, each drawn by a single animal.

The chariots themselves were large and gorgeously decorated. In each was seated a female Martian loaded with metal ornaments, jewels, silks, and furs. On the back of each of the harnessed beasts was perched a young Martian driver. Like the animals ridden by the warriors, the heavier draft animals were not controlled by reins and a bridle, but were guided by some kind of telepathic mind-control technique.

This telepathic power is greatly developed in all Martians, and accounts for their simple language and the relatively few spoken words exchanged even in long conversations. It is the universal language of Mars, through which the higher and lower animals of this world of paradoxes are able to communicate to a greater or lesser extent, depending on the intellect of the species and the development of the individual.

As the vehicles formed into a single-file line of march, Sola and I climbed into an empty chariot and we followed along toward the point where I had entered the city the day before. At the head of the caravan rode some two hundred warriors, five abreast, and a like number brought up the rear, while twenty-five or thirty outriders flanked us on either side.

Every one but myself—men, women, and children—was heavily armed, and at the tail of each chariot trotted a Martian hound, my own beast following closely behind ours. Our way led out across the valley in front of the city, through the hills, and down into the dead sea bottom where I had found the incubator. The incubator, as it turned out, was the destination of our journey this day, and as the entire cavalcade broke into a mad gallop as soon as we reached the level expanse of sea bottom, we were soon within sight of our goal.

When we arrived, the chariots were parked with military precision on the four sides of the enclosure, and six warriors, headed by the enormous chieftain, and including Tars Tarkas and other lesser chiefs, dismounted and advanced to the nearest wall. I could see Tars Tarkas explaining something to the principal chieftain, whose name, by the way, was as nearly as I can translate it into English, Lorquas Ptomel, Jed, jed being his title.

I soon found out the subject of their conversation, as Tars Tarkas signed for me to join him. I had by this time mastered the intricacies of walking under Martian conditions, and quickly responded to his command. I saw that all but a very few eggs had hatched, the incubator being fairly alive with the hideous little devils. They ranged in height from three to four feet, and were moving restlessly inside the enclosure like they were searching for food.

Lorquas Ptomel turned to his warriors and gave a few words of command related to the incubator. I was permitted to remain close and watch them break an opening through the wall large enough to permit the recently hatched Martians to get out.

On either side of this opening the women and the younger Martians, both male and female, formed two solid walls leading out through the chariots and quite a way into the plain beyond.

Between these walls the little Martians scampered, wild as deer. They were allowed to run the full length of the aisle, where they were captured one at a time at the end. The last in the line capturing the first little one to reach the end of the gauntlet, her opposite in the line capturing the second, and so on until all the little fellows had left the enclosure and had been claimed. As the women and youths caught the hatchlings they fell out of line and returned to their chariots.

I saw that the ceremony, if it could be dignified by such a name, was over, and I soon found Sola in our chariot with a hideous little green creature held tightly in her arms.

The work of rearing green young Martians consists solely of teaching them to talk and to use the weapons of warfare which they are loaded down with from the very first year of their lives. Coming from eggs in which they have incubated for five years, they come into the world almost perfectly developed except in size. Because they are unknown to their mothers, who in turn would have difficulty in pointing out the fathers with any degree of accuracy, they are the common children of the community, and their education is left to the females who chance to capture them as they leave the incubator.

Their foster mothers may not even have had an egg in the incubator, as was the case with Sola. But this counts for little among the green

Martians, as parental love is as unknown to them as it is common among us. I believe this ages-old, horrible system causes the loss of the finer feelings and higher human instincts among these poor creatures. From birth they do not know love from either father or mother; they do not know the meaning of the word home; they are taught that they are only allowed to survive until they can demonstrate by their physique and ferocity that they are fit to live. If they prove deformed or defective in any way they are promptly shot.

I do not mean that the adult Martians are intentionally cruel to the young, but theirs is a hard and pitiless struggle for existence on a dying planet, where the natural resources have dwindled to a point where the support of each additional life means an added tax on the whole community. By careful selection, they rear only the hardiest specimens of each species, and with almost supernatural foresight they regulate the birth rate to merely offset the losses by death.

Each adult Martian female brings forth about thirteen eggs each year, and those which meet the size, weight, and specific gravity tests are hidden in the recesses of some underground vault where the temperature is too low for incubation. Every year these eggs are carefully examined, and all but one hundred of the most perfect are destroyed. At the end of five years, five hundred perfect eggs have been chosen from the thousands brought forth. These are then placed in the incubators to be hatched by the sun's rays after a period of another five years. The incubators are built in remote areas where there is little chance of their being discovered and destroyed by rival tribes.

My little community of green Martians formed a part of a larger tribe composed of some thirty thousand souls. They roamed an enormous tract of arid and semi-arid land with their permanent headquarters at the city of Thark in the southwest corner of this district, near the crossing of two of the so-called Martian canals.

After our return to the temporary camp in the dead city, Sola's duties were now doubled. She had to care for the young Martian as well as me, but neither one of us required much attention, and since we were both about equally advanced in Martian education, Sola took it upon herself to train us together.

Her new prize was a male about four feet tall, very strong and physically perfect. He learned quickly, and we had a great deal of amusement, at least I did, over the rivalry we displayed. The Martian language, as I have said, is extremely simple, and in a week I could make all my wants known and understand nearly everything that was said to me. Likewise, under Sola's training, I developed my telepathic powers so that I could sense practically everything that went on around me.

What surprised Sola most about me was that while I could easily catch telepathic messages from others, and often when they were not intended for me, no one could read anything from my mind. At first this bothered me, but later I was pleased, as it gave me a definite advantage over the Martians.

A Beautiful Captive
from the Sky

After returning to camp from the incubator ceremony we set off toward their permanent city but had barely entered open ground when we were ordered back. As though trained for years in this particular maneuver, the green Martians melted like mist into the spacious doorways of the nearby buildings, until, in less than three minutes, the entire cavalcade of chariots, mastodons and mounted warriors was nowhere to be seen.

Sola and I entered a building, and wishing to see what had caused the sudden retreat, went to an upper floor window and looked out over the valley. There I saw the reason—a huge aircraft, long, low, and painted gray, floated slowly over the nearest hill! Following it came another, and another, and another, until twenty of them sailed slowly and majestically toward us.

Each carried a strange banner swung from stem to stern, and each had some odd device painted on its bow that gleamed in the sunlight and showed plainly even at a distance. I could see figures crowding the decks and upper works of the ships. Whether they had discovered us or simply were looking at the deserted city I could not say, but in any event they received a rude reception. Suddenly the green Martian warriors fired almost all of their weapons at the peacefully advancing airships.

Instantly the scene changed. The front vessel swung broadside to us, and bringing her guns into play, returned our fire, at the same time moving parallel to our front for a short distance and then turning away from us. The other vessels followed in her wake, each one opening up on us as she swung into position. Our own fire never diminished—I had never seen such deadly accuracy—it seemed as though a little figure on one of their ships dropped for every one of our shots, while their banners and upper works dissolved in spurts of flame as our bullets mowed through them.

The return fire from the vessels was wild, and twenty minutes after the first volley the great fleet turned off to escape. Several of the craft were severely damaged and seemed barely controlled by what was left of their crews. Our warriors followed the retreating fleet with continuous deadly fire.

One by one, however, the ships managed to dip below the crests of the outlying hills until only one barely moving craft was in sight. This one had received the brunt of our fire and seemed to be entirely unmanned—not a moving figure was visible on her decks. Slowly she swung from her course, circling back toward us in an erratic and pitiful manner. Instantly the warriors ceased firing, for it was quite apparent that the vessel was helpless, and far from being in a position to inflict harm on us, she could not even get away.

As she neared the city the warriors rushed out to meet her, but it was plain that she still was too high for them to reach her decks. From my viewing point in the window I could see the bodies of her crew strewn about, although I could not make out what manner of creatures they might be. Not a sign of life was visible as she drifted slowly in our direction.

She was floating some fifty feet above the ground, followed by about one hundred of our warriors. I watched the progress of the chase and saw a number of warriors gallop ahead, dismount and enter the building the ship was approaching.

As the craft neared the building, and just before she struck, the Martian warriors swarmed onto her from the windows, and with their long spears eased the shock of the collision. In a few moments they had thrown out grappling hooks and the big ship was being hauled down to the ground.

After securing her, they swarmed over the sides and searched the vessel from stem to stern. I could see them examining the dead sailors, evidently for signs of life, and presently a party of them appeared from below dragging a little struggling figure. The creature was considerably less than half as tall as the green Martian warriors and I guessed it was some new and strange Martian monster.

They moved their prisoner to the ground and then started to ransack the vessel. This operation required several hours, during which time a number of the chariots were requisitioned to transport the loot, which consisted of arms, ammunition, silks, furs, jewels, and a quantity of solid foods and liquids, including many casks of water, the first I had seen since my arrival on Mars.

After the last load had been removed, the warriors towed the craft out into the valley. The last warrior to leave set her on fire as he swung over the side. Just as he landed the ropes were released, and the great warship, lightened by the removal of the loot, soared majestically into the air, her decks a mass of roaring flames.

Slowly she drifted, rising higher and higher as the flames ate away her wooden parts and diminished her weight. I watched her for hours, until finally she was lost in the distance. The sight was awe-inspiring as I contemplated this mighty floating funeral pyre, drifting unguided through the lonely wastes of the Martian heavens.

Unaccountably depressed, I slowly descended to the street. The scene I had witnessed seemed to mark the defeat of people similar to me, rather than the routing by our green warriors of a horde of creatures similar to themselves. I could not understand the vision in my mind, but somehow I felt a strange yearning toward these unknown people. Hope surged through me that the fleet would return and demand a reckoning from these green warriors who had so ruthlessly attacked it.

Close at my heel, in his now accustomed place, followed Woola, the hound, and as I emerged on the street Sola rushed up to me with news that the homeward march was given up for the day. As we entered the plaza a sight met my eyes which filled me with a great surge of mingled hope, fear, exultation, and depression—I caught a glimpse of the prisoner as she was being roughly dragged into a nearby building by a couple of green Martian females.

The sight that met my eyes was of a slender, girlish figure, similar in every detail to the earthly women of my past life. She did not see me at first, but just as she was disappearing into the building she turned and her eyes met mine. Her face was oval and beautiful; her features were finely chiseled and exquisite; her eyes large and lustrous and on her head was a mass of coal black, wavy hair. Her skin was a light reddish copper color, against which the crimson glow of her cheeks and the ruby of her beautifully molded lips shone with a strangely enhancing effect. Except for her decorative ornaments and trappings she was as naked as the green Martians who accompanied her. I thought to myself that no apparel could have enhanced the beauty of her perfect figure.

As her gaze met mine her eyes opened wide in astonishment. For just a moment we gazed at each other, and then her look of hope and renewed courage faded to utter dejection. Though ignorant of Martian customs, I felt that she had made an appeal for protection that my ignorance had prevented me from answering. She was then dragged out of my sight into the depths of the building.

CHAPTER 9

I Learn the Language

As I recovered from this scene I glanced at Sola, who had witnessed the encounter, and I was surprised to note a strange look on her usually expressionless face. What her thoughts were I did not know, nor could I ask, for as yet I had learned but little of the Martian tongue—only enough for my daily needs.

As I reached our building a strange surprise awaited me. A warrior approached bearing the arms, ornaments, and full equipment of a highly placed chieftain. These he presented to me with a few mumbled words, but his bearing was respectful. Sola soon remodeled these trappings to fit my lesser proportions, and afterward I went out garbed in all the splendor of a green Martian warrior.

From then on Sola instructed me in the mysteries of their various weapons and with the

Martian young I spent several hours each day practicing on the plaza. Since I was familiar with similar earthly weapons, I was an unusually good pupil, and I progressed in a satisfactory manner.

The green Martian women conducted both my training and that of the young Martians. They not only take care of the education of the young in the arts of defense and offense, but are also the skilled laborers who produce every manufactured article made by the green Martians. They make the powder, cartridges, and firearms—in fact everything of value is produced by the females. In time of actual warfare they form a part of the reserves, and when the necessity arises, fight with even greater intelligence and ferocity than the men.

The men are trained in the higher branches of the art of war—in strategy and maneuvers. They make the laws as they are needed—a new law for each emergency. Though customs have been handed down by ages of repetition, the punishment for ignoring a custom is a matter for individual treatment by a jury of the culprit's peers. In one respect, at least, the green Martians are a happy people—they have no lawyers.

I did not see the prisoner again for several days but then caught a fleeting glimpse of her as she was being taken to the audience chamber where I first met with Lorquas Ptomel. I observed that the prisoner exchanged words with her guards, and this convinced me that they spoke a common language. With this added incentive I nearly drove Sola crazy with my demands to continue my language education. In just a few more days I mastered the Martian tongue well enough to carry on a passable conversation and to understand practically all that I heard.

At this time, we shared our sleeping quarters with three additional females and two of the recently hatched young. After the young retired for the night it was customary for the adults to carry on a quiet conversation before lapsing into sleep, and now that I could understand their language I was a keen listener, although I never offered any remarks myself.

On the night following the prisoner's visit to the audience chamber I listened very carefully. I was afraid to question Sola about the beautiful captive, as I could not help recall the strange expression on her face after my first encounter with the prisoner. If she was jealous I could not say, but I felt it safer to pretend indifference until I learned more of Sola's attitude toward the beautiful red lady.

Sarkoja, one of the older women who shared our apartment, had been present in the audience chamber as one of the captive's guards, and it was toward her the question turned.

"When," asked one of the women, "will we

enjoy the death agonies of the red one? Or does Lorquas Ptomel, Jed, intend holding her for ransom?"

"They have decided to carry her with us back to Thark, and exhibit her last agonies at the Great Games and for Tal Hajus's entertainment," replied Sarkoja.

"What will be the manner of her death?" inquired Sola. "She is very small and very beautiful, I had hoped that they would hold her for ransom."

Sarkoja and the other women grunted angrily at this evidence of weakness on the part of Sola. "It is sad, Sola, that you were not born a million years ago when all the hollows of the land were filled with water, and the peoples were as soft as the stuff they sailed their boats on," snapped Sarkoja. "In our day we have progressed to a point where such thoughts mark weakness. It will not be good for you if Tars Tarkas learns that you hold such sentiments. I doubt that he would care to trust someone like you with the responsibilities of maternity."

"I see nothing wrong with my expression of interest in this red woman. She has never harmed us; it is only the men of her kind who make war on us and then only after they have been provoked. I have always thought that their attitude toward us is only the reflection of our attitude toward them. They live at peace with all their fellow creatures, except when duty calls on them to make war, but we are at peace with no one. We war among our own kind as well as on the red men. Even in our own little communities we fight among ourselves. Oh, it is one continual, awful period of bloodshed from the time we break the shell until we gladly embrace the bosom of the river of mystery, the dark and ancient River Iss which carries us to an unknown, but at least no more frightful and terrible existence. Fortunate indeed are the ones who meet their end in an early death. Say what you please to Tars Tarkas, he can give me no worse fate than a continuation of the horrible existence we are forced to lead in this life!"

This wild outbreak on the part of Sola surprised and shocked the other women. But after only a few more words they all lapsed into silence and were soon asleep. One thing the episode had accomplished was to assure me of Sola's friendliness toward the poor girl, and also to convince me that I had been extremely fortunate in falling into her hands rather than those of some other female. I knew that she was fond of me, and now that I had discovered that she hated cruelty and violence, I was confident that she would help the girl and me escape.

I did not know if we would be escaping to a better situation, but I was willing to take my chances among people fashioned after my own mold rather than to remain among the blood-thirsty green men. I decided I would soon take Sola into my confidence and ask for her help. I then wrapped myself up in my silks and furs and slept the dreamless and refreshing sleep of Mars.

CHAPTER 10

Champion and Chief

I was up early the next morning ready to do some exploring. Sola told me that I was free to go where I pleased as long as I did not try to leave the city. She did warn me, however, about going out unarmed, reminding me of the great white apes. Sola also explained that Woola would tag along with me and prevent any escape. She said not to stir up Woola's fierce nature by getting too close to the forbidden edge of the city.

I had chosen a new street to explore when I suddenly found myself at the city limits. In front of me were low hills pierced by narrow and inviting valleys. I longed to explore this country and check out the landscape.

It occurred to me that this would be a good time to test Woola's loyalties. I was convinced that the brute cared for me. I had seen more evidence of affection in him than in any other

Martian, man or beast. I was sure that gratitude for my twice saving his life would more than outweigh his loyalty to his cruel masters.

As I approached the boundary line Woola ran anxiously in front of me. His expression was pleading rather than ferocious, and he did not show his tusks or utter his terrible warning growl. Denied earthly friendship and companionship, I had developed considerable affection for this animal. I had never before petted him, but now I sat on the ground and put my arms around his heavy neck and stroked him. I talked to him in my newly acquired Martian tongue as I would talk to my hound at home—as I would have talked to any other friend among the lower animals. His response to this display of affection was remarkable.

He threw himself on his back and almost wallowed at my feet. He jumped up, knocking me on the ground, and then wriggled and squirmed around me like a playful puppy. I could not resist the humor of the spectacle, and I rocked back and forth in the first laughter that had passed my lips in many days.

My laughter frightened Woola, his antics ceased and he crawled pitifully toward me, poking his ugly head into my lap. Then I remembered what laughter signified on Mars—torture, suffering, and death. Quieting myself, I rubbed the poor old fellow's head and back, talked to

him for a few minutes, and then in a commanding tone ordered him to follow me, and started
for the hills.

There was no further question of authority
between us. Woola was my devoted slave from
that moment on, and I was his master. My walk
took just a few minutes, and as I stood at the
summit of the first hill, I saw still other hills
stretching off toward the north, and rising, one
range above another, until lost in the distant
mountains.

My morning's walk was important because
while Tars Tarkas relied on Woola for my safekeeping, I now knew that, while theoretically a
prisoner, I was virtually free. I quickly returned to
the city limits and decided not to leave my
assigned area again until I was ready to venture
out for good.

When we returned to the plaza I got my
third glimpse of the captive girl. She was standing
with her guards in front of the audience chamber
building. I stopped to watch as Lorquas Ptomel
and his attendants approached the building and,
signaling the guards to follow with the prisoner,
entered. Remembering that I was a favored char-
acter, and convinced that the warriors thought I
did not know their language well, I followed
behind them.

The council squatted on the rostrum, while
the prisoner and her two guards stood below. I

saw that one was Sarkoja and that when she held the captive, she sank her fingers into the poor girl's flesh, or twisted her arm in a most painful manner. She seemed to be venting all the hatred, cruelty, and spite of her nine hundred years on the poor defenseless girl.

As Lorquas Ptomel raised his eyes to address the prisoner they fell on me and he turned to Tars Tarkas. Tars Tarkas made some reply I could not catch, but which caused Lorquas Ptomel to smile, and they paid no further attention to me.

"What is your name?" demanded Lorquas Ptomel, addressing the prisoner.

"Dejah Thoris, daughter of Mors Kajak of Helium."

"And the nature of your expedition?"

"It was a purely scientific research party sent out by my father's father, the Jeddak of Helium, to re-chart the air currents, and to take atmospheric density tests," replied the fair prisoner, in a low, well-modulated voice.

"We were unprepared for battle because we were on a peaceful mission as our banners and the colors of our craft displayed. The work we were doing was as much in your interests as in ours, for you know full well that if it were not for our labors and the fruits of our scientific operations there would not be enough air or water on Mars to support a single life. For ages we have maintained the air and water supply without any noticeable loss, and we have done this in the face of the brutal and ignorant interference of you green men.

"Why, oh, why will you not learn to live in peace with us? Must you go to your final extinction after advancing so little above the dumb brutes that serve you? You are people without written language, without art, without homes, without love. You are the victims of eons of this horrible 'community' idea. Owning everything in common, even your women and children, has resulted in your owning nothing in common. You hate each other as much as you hate everything else. Come back to the ways of our common ancestors; come back to the light of kindness and fellowship. The way is open; you will find the hands of the red men stretched out to aid you. Working together we could do so much more to rebuild our dying planet. The granddaughter of the mightiest of the red jeddaks has asked you. Will you join us?"

Lorquas Ptomel and the warriors sat looking silently and intently at the young woman for several moments after she ceased speaking. What was passing in their minds no one could know, but I believe that they were moved, and if one man among them had been strong enough to rise above custom, that moment would have marked a new and mighty era for Mars.

I saw Tars Tarkas rise, and on his face was an

expression I had never seen on a green Martian warrior. It showed an inward and mighty battle within himself, with his upbringing, with age-old custom, and as he opened his mouth to speak, a look almost of kindness momentarily lit up his fierce and terrible face.

What words might have fallen from his lips were never spoken, as just then a young warrior, sensing the trend of thought among the older men, leaped down from the steps of the rostrum, and struck the captive across the face! She fell to the floor, and he placed his foot on her prostrate form and turned to the assembled council and broke into peals of horrid, mirthless laughter.

For an instant I thought Tars Tarkas would strike him dead, and Lorquas Ptomel did not look too favorably on the brute either, but the mood passed, their old attitude returned, and they smiled. It was meaningful, however, that they did not laugh aloud, for the brute's act was a sidesplitting joke according to the principles that rule green Martian humor.

Though I have taken moments to write down what occurred as that blow fell does not mean that I was inactive. I think I must have sensed something of what was coming, for I realize now that I was crouched ready to spring as I saw the blow aimed at her beautiful, upturned, pleading face, and before the hand descended I was halfway across the hall.

Scarcely had his hideous laugh sounded out, when I was on him! The brute was twelve feet in height and armed to the teeth, but I believe that I could have handled the whole roomful in my rage. Springing upward, I struck him full in the face as he turned at my warning cry. Then as he drew his sword I drew mine and jumped up on his chest, hooking one leg over the butt of his pistol and grasping one of his huge tusks with my left hand while I slashed and cut and punched with my right.

He could not use his sword because I was too close to him, nor could he draw his pistol, which he attempted to do in direct opposition to Martian custom. This quaint rule says that you may not fight a fellow warrior in private combat with anything other than the weapon with which you are attacked. In fact he could do nothing but make a wild and futile attempt to shake me off. With all his immense bulk he was not much stronger than I, and it was just a moment or two before he sank, bleeding and lifeless, to the floor.

Dejah Thoris was watching the battle with wide, staring eyes. When I got to my feet I lifted her in my arms and carried her to one of the benches at the side of the room. Again, no one interfered with me, and tearing a piece of silk from my cape, I tried to stop the flow of blood from her nostrils. I was soon successful; her injuries were little more than an ordinary nosebleed, and when she could speak she placed her hand on my arm and looked into my eyes and said: "Why did you do that? You who refused me even friendly recognition in the first hour of my peril! And now you risk your life and kill one of your companions for my sake. I cannot understand. What strange manner of man are you? You associate with the green men, though your form is that of my race, while your color is little darker than the white ape. Tell me, are you human, or are you more than human?"

"It is a strange tale," I replied, "too long to attempt to tell you now. I almost do not believe the story myself and I fear how you will react when you hear it. For the present, let me say that I am your friend, and so far as our captors will permit, I am your protector and your servant."

"Then you too are a prisoner? But why do you wear the arms and the regalia of a Tharkian chieftain? What is your name? Where is your country?"

"Yes, Dejah Thoris, I too am a prisoner. My name is John Carter, and I claim Virginia, one of the United States of America, Earth, as my home. But why I am permitted to wear arms I do not know, nor was I aware that my regalia was that of a chieftain."

We were interrupted by the approach of one of the warriors, bearing arms and ornaments, and in a flash one of her questions was answered and a puzzle cleared. I saw that the body of the warrior I had just killed had been stripped, and I read in the respectful attitude of the warrior who brought me these trophies the same demeanor as that displayed by the other one who brought me my original equipment. Now, for the first time, I realized that my punch, in my first fight in the audience chamber the other day, had resulted in the death of my adversary.

The reason for the attitude displayed toward me was now apparent. I had won my spurs, so to speak, and in the crude justice that marks Martian dealings, I was given the honors due a conqueror. I was awarded the trappings and the position of the man I killed. In truth, I had become a Martian chieftain after the prior fight, and this had gained me my freedom and my toleration in the audience chamber.

As I turned to receive the dead warrior's goods I noticed that Tars Tarkas and several others had pushed toward us. Finally he addressed me: "You speak the tongue of Barsoom quite readily for one who was deaf and dumb to us a few short days ago. Where did you learn it, John Carter?"

"You, yourself, are responsible, Tars Tarkas. You furnished me with an instructor of remarkable ability. I have to thank Sola for my learning."

"She has done well, but your education in other respects needs considerable polish. Do you know what your aggression would have cost you if you failed to kill either of the two chieftains whose metal you now wear?"

"I presume that if I had failed to kill one, he would have killed me," I answered, smiling.

"No, you are wrong. Only in the last extremity of self-defense would a Martian warrior kill a prisoner. We like to save them for other purposes," and his face implied possibilities that were not pleasant to think about.

"Only one thing can save you now," he continued. "Should you, in recognition of your remarkable valor, ferocity, and prowess, be considered by Tal Hajus, our mighty and most ferocious ruler, as worthy of his service you may be taken into our community and become a full-fledged Tharkian. Until we reach the headquarters of Tal Hajus it is the will of Lorquas Ptomel that you be accorded the respect your acts have earned you. You will be treated as a Tharkian chieftain, but you must not forget that every chief who outranks you is responsible for your safe delivery. I have spoken."

"I hear you, Tars Tarkas. As you know I am not of Barsoom. Your ways are not my ways, and I can only act in the future as I have in the past— controlled by my conscience and guided by the standards of my own people. If you will leave me alone I will go in peace, but if not, let the individual Barsoomians with whom I must deal either respect my rights as a stranger among you, or take whatever consequences may occur. Of one thing let us be sure, whatever may be your ultimate intentions toward this unfortunate young woman, whoever would offer her injury or insult in the future must figure on making a full accounting to me. I understand that you think little of all sentiments of generosity and kindness, but I do not, and I can convince your best warrior that these characteristics are not incompatible with an ability to fight."

Ordinarily I am not given to long speeches but, as I started talking, I guessed what would strike an answering chord in the green Martians. I was not wrong, for my speech impressed them, and their attitude toward me afterward was even more respectful. Tars Tarkas himself seemed pleased with my reply.

I now turned my attention to Dejah Thoris, and assisting her to her feet I turned with her toward the exit, ignoring her guardians as well as the inquiring glances of the chieftains. I was now a chieftain! Well, then, I would assume the responsibilities of one. No one bothered us, and so Dejah Thoris, Princess of Helium, and John Carter, gentleman of Virginia, followed by the faithful Woola, passed in silence from the audience chamber of Lorquas Ptomel, Jed among the Tharks of Barsoom.

CHAPTER 11

With Dejah Thoris

As we reached the open, the two female guards detailed to watch over Dejah Thoris hurried up and attempted to assume custody of her once again. The poor child shrank against me and I felt her hands fold tightly over my arm. Waving the women away, I informed them that Sola would attend the captive from now on, and I further warned Sarkoja that any more of her cruel attentions toward Dejah Thoris would result in Sarkoja's painful demise. Sarkoja gave us an ugly look and departed to hatch up more evil plots against us.

I found Sola and told her to guard Dejah Thoris. I directed her to find other quarters away from Sarkoja, and I informed her that I would take up my quarters among the men.

Sola glanced at the new adornments I carried. "You are a great chieftain now, John

Carter," she said, "and I must do your bidding. The man whose metal you carry was young, but he was a great warrior, and had by his promotions and kills won his way close to the rank of Tars Tarkas. Our chief, as you know, is second only to Lorquas Ptomel. You are eleventh, there are but ten chieftains in this community who outrank you in prowess."

"And if I should kill Lorquas Ptomel?" I asked.

"You would be first, John Carter, but you may only win that honor if the entire council directed that Lorquas Ptomel meet you in combat. Another way would be if he were to attack you, you could then kill him in self-defense, and in that way, win first place."

I laughed, and changed the subject. I had no particular desire to kill Lorquas Ptomel, and even less to be a jed among the Tharks.

I accompanied Sola and Dejah Thoris in a search for new quarters, which we found in a building of far more extravagant architecture than our former rooms. Here we also found real sleeping apartments with ancient beds swinging from enormous gold chains attached to the marble ceilings. The decoration of the walls was most elaborate, and unlike the murals in the other buildings, these portrayed many human figures. They were people like myself, and of a much lighter color than Dejah Thoris. They were clad in graceful, flowing robes, highly ornamented with metal and jewels, and their glossy hair was of a beautiful golden and reddish bronze. The men were beardless and only a few wore arms. The scenes depicted a fair-skinned, fair-haired people at play.

Dejah Thoris clasped her hands with delight as she gazed on these magnificent works of art, made by a people long extinct, while Sola, on the other hand, apparently did not see them.

We decided to use this room, on the second floor and overlooking the plaza, for Dejah Thoris and Sola, and another room for the cooking and supplies. I then sent Sola to bring the bedding and such food and utensils as she might need, telling her that I would guard Dejah Thoris until her return.

As Sola departed, Dejah Thoris turned to me with a faint smile. "And where would your prisoner escape to, unless it was to follow you and beg for your protection, and ask your pardon for the cruel thoughts she has held against you these past few days?"

"You are right, Dejah Thoris, there is no escape for either of us unless we go together."

"I heard your challenge to the creature you call Tars Tarkas," she said, "and I think I understand your position among these people, but what I cannot understand is your statement that you are not from Barsoom.

"In the name of my first ancestor, where are you from? You are like my people, and yet so different. You speak my language, and yet I heard you tell Tars Tarkas that you had only learned it recently. All Barsoomians speak the same tongue from the ice-clad south to the ice-clad north, though their written languages differ. Only in the Valley Dor, where the River Iss empties into the lost Sea of Korus, is there supposed to be a different language spoken. Do not tell me that you have returned from there! They would kill you horribly if that were true! Tell me it is not!"

Her eyes were filled with a strange, weird light. Her voice was pleading, and her hands reached up to my chest and pressed against me as though to wring a denial from my very heart.

"I do not know your customs, Dejah Thoris, but in my own Virginia a gentleman does not lie to save himself. I am not from the Valley Dor. I have never seen the mysterious River Iss. The lost Sea of Korus is still lost, so far as I am concerned. Do you believe me?"

And then it struck me that I was very anxious that she believe me. Why should I care what she thought? I looked down at her, at her beautiful face looking back at me, and her wonderful eyes opening up the very depth of her soul—and as my eyes met hers I knew why, and—I shuddered.

A similar wave of feeling seemed to stir in her. She drew away from me with a sigh, and with her earnest, beautiful face turned up to mine, she whispered, "I believe you, John Carter. I do not know what a 'gentleman' is, nor have I ever heard before of Virginia. But on Barsoom no man lies! If he does not wish to speak the truth he is silent. Where is this country of Virginia, John Carter?" she asked, and it seemed that this fair name of my fair land had never sounded more beautiful than as it fell from those perfect lips on that far-gone day.

"I am of another world," I answered, "the planet Earth, which revolves around our common sun closer than the orbit of your Barsoom, which we know as Mars. How I came here I cannot tell you, for I do not know. But here I am, and since my presence has permitted me to serve Dejah Thoris I am so very glad that I am here."

She gazed at me with troubled eyes. I knew that it was difficult to believe my statement but finally she smiled, and said, "I shall have to believe even though I cannot understand. I can see that you are not of the Barsoom of today. You are like us, yet different—but why should I trouble my poor head with such a problem, when my heart tells me that I believe because I wish to believe!"

It was good logic, good, earthly, feminine logic, and if it satisfied her I certainly could pick no flaws in it. As a matter of fact, it was about the only kind of logic that could be brought to bear on my problem. We then began a general conversation, asking and answering many questions on each side. She was curious to learn of the customs of my people and displayed a remarkable knowledge of events on Earth.

When I questioned her on this familiarity with earthly things she laughed, and cried out, "Why, every school boy on Barsoom knows the geography, and much concerning the animals and plants, as well as the history of your planet fully as well as he knows his own land. We are able to see everything that takes place on Earth, as you call it. Is it not hanging there in the heavens in plain sight?"

This baffled me as much as my statements had puzzled her. She then explained the telescopic instruments her people had used for ages. These permit the user to show on a screen a perfect image of what is transpiring on any planet of our solar system. These pictures are so perfect in detail that, when photographed and enlarged, objects no greater than a blade of grass are recognizable.

"If you are so familiar with earthly things," I asked, "why is it that you do not recognize me as an inhabitant of that planet?"

She smiled again as one might smile in bored discussion with a questioning child.

"Because, John Carter, nearly every planet with atmospheric conditions remotely similar to those of Barsoom, shows forms of animal life almost identical with you and me. Furthermore, Earthmen, almost without exception, cover their bodies with strange, unsightly pieces of cloth, and their heads with hideous contraptions. But you were entirely unadorned when found by the Tharkian warriors.

"The fact that you wore no ornaments is a strong proof of your un-Barsoomian origin, while the absence of ugly cloth coverings might cause a doubt as to your earthliness."

I then told her of my departure from Earth, explaining that my body, back there in the cave, lay fully clothed in all the 'strange' garments of ordinary Earthlings. At this point Sola returned with our few belongings and her young Martian hatchling, who, of course, would have to share the quarters with the two women.

Sola asked us if we had talked with anyone during her absence, and seemed surprised when we answered in the negative. She told us she had seen Sarkoja coming down the stairs when she was on her way up. We decided that Sarkoja must have been eavesdropping, but we could not think of anything important we discussed so we dismissed the matter.

Dejah Thoris and I then continued our examination of the architecture and decorations of the beautiful chambers we were occupying. She told me that these people had flourished here over a hundred thousand years before. They were the ancestors of her race, but had mixed with the other races of early Martians.

These different races of the higher Martians had joined in alliance as the Martian seas dried up and the land became more barren and hostile. This forced them to seek the few and diminishing fertile areas and to defend themselves against the wild hordes of green men.

Ages of close relationship and intermarrying resulted in Dejah Thoris's present race of red men. During the ages of hardships and incessant conflict with the green men, much of the high civilization and many of the arts of the Martians had been lost. But the new discoveries of today's red race have made up for much that lies permanently buried with the ancient Barsoomians. Those ancient Martians had been a highly cultivated and literary race, but during the centuries of readjustment their advancement stopped and practically all their archives, records, and literature were lost.

Dejah Thoris related many interesting facts and legends concerning this lost race of noble and kindly people. She said that this city of Korad, our present location, was supposed to have been a center of commerce and culture. It had been built on a beautiful, natural harbor, landlocked by magnificent hills. The little valley on the west front of the city was all that remained of the harbor, while the pass through the hills to the old sea bottom had been the channel through which the shipping passed up to the city's gates.

We were so engrossed in our conversation and exploration that it was late afternoon before we realized it. A messenger brought me back to reality with a summons from Lorquas Ptomel. Bidding the females farewell, and commanding Woola to remain on guard, I quickly walked to the audience chamber, where I found Lorquas Ptomel and Tars Tarkas.

A Prisoner with Power

As I entered, Lorquas Ptomel told me to advance, and fixing his hideous eyes on me, said, "You have been with us a few days, yet during that time you have won a high position among us. Be that as it may, you are not one of us and we know you owe us no loyalty.

"Your position is a strange one; you are a prisoner and yet you give commands which must be obeyed. You are an alien and yet you are a Tharkian chieftain. You are half our size and yet you can kill a mighty warrior with one blow of your fist. And now we have a report that you have been plotting to escape with the red prisoner. A prisoner who, from her own admission, half believes you are returned from the Valley Dor. If proved, either one of these accusations would be sufficient grounds for your execution, but we are a just people and you shall have a trial on our return to the city of Thark, if Tal Hajus so commands.

"But," he continued, in his fierce guttural tones, "if you run off with the red girl it is I who will have to account to Tal Hajus and either demonstrate my right to command, or the metal from my dead carcass will go to a better man, for such is the custom of the Tharks.

"If you were dead, John Carter, I would be glad. However, only under two conditions may you be killed without orders from Tal Hajus: if you should attack one of us, we could kill you in self-defense, or, if you were caught while attempting to escape.

"As a matter of justice I must warn you that we only await one of these two excuses for ridding ourselves of so great a responsibility. The safe delivery of the red girl to Tal Hajus is of the greatest importance. Not in a thousand years have the Tharks made such a capture. She is the granddaughter of the greatest of the red jeddaks, who is also our bitterest enemy. The red girl told us that we were without the softer feelings and attitudes of humanity, but we are a just and truthful race. I have spoken. You may go."

Turning, I left the audience chamber. So this was the beginning of Sarkoja's plot. I knew that no one else could be responsible for the report that had reached Lorquas Ptomel's ears so quickly. Sarkoja was Tars Tarkas's oldest and most trusted female. As such, she was a power behind the throne, for no other warrior had more of Lorquas Ptomel's confidence than Tars Tarkas.

However, instead of chasing thoughts of escape from my mind, my audience with Lorquas Ptomel only served to make me concentrate more fully on this subject. I was convinced that some horrible fate awaited Dejah Thoris when we reached Tal Hajus's headquarters and the necessity of escape was uppermost on my mind.

As described by Sola, this monster, Tal Hajus, was the personification of cruelty and brutality. Cold, cunning, calculating—he was also, in marked contrast to most of the other green men, a slave to sexual passion which the waning demands for procreation on their dying planet has almost eliminated in Martian behavior. The thought that the beautiful Dejah Thoris might fall into the clutches of this brute of a ruler caused me to break out in a cold sweat.

As I wandered in the plaza lost in my gloom, Tars Tarkas approached me on his way from the audience chamber. He greeted me as though we had not just parted a few moments before.

"Where are your quarters, John Carter?"

"I have not selected any, yet," I replied. "It seemed best that I find a place either by myself or among the other warriors, and I was awaiting an opportunity to ask your advice. As you know," and I smiled, "I am not yet familiar with all the customs of the Tharks."

"Come with me," he directed, and together we moved off across the plaza to a building next to the one occupied by Sola and her charges.

"My quarters are on the first floor of this building," he said, "and the second floor is fully occupied by my warriors, but the third floor and the floors above are vacant. You may take your choice of these.

"I understand that you have given up your woman to the red prisoner. Well, as you have said, your ways are not our ways, but you can fight well enough to do as you please, and so, if you wish to give your woman to a captive, it is your own affair. But as a chieftain, you should have servants, and in accordance with our customs you may select any or all the females from the attendants of the chieftains whose metal you now wear."

I thanked him, but assured him that I could get along very nicely without assistance except in the matter of preparing food, and so he promised to send me women for this purpose. After he left, I entered the building and went up the stairs to the third floor. The beautiful works of art in the other building were repeated in this one, and I was soon lost in a tour of investigation and discovery.

I finally chose a front room on the third floor, near Dejah Thoris, whose apartment was on the second floor of the adjoining building. I thought I could rig up some means of communication where she might signal me in case of need.

Next to my sleeping apartment were baths, dressing rooms, and other sleeping and living apartments. The windows of the back rooms overlooked an enormous court overgrown with the yellow, moss-like vegetation. Numerous fountains, statues, and benches bore witness to the beauty the court must have presented in ancient times.

One could easily picture the gorgeous foliage of the luxuriant Martian vegetation that once filled this scene with life and color. I imagined the graceful figures of the beautiful women, the handsome men, the happy frolicking children— all in sunlight, happiness, and peace. It was difficult to realize that they had disappeared into ages of darkness, cruelty, and ignorance. But now the inherited instincts of their culture had risen once more in the final red race now dominant on Mars.

My thoughts were cut short by the entry of several young females bearing loads of weapons, silks, furs, jewels, cooking utensils, and casks of food and drink, including considerable loot from the aircraft. All this had been the property of the two chieftains I had killed, and now, by the customs of the Tharks, had become mine. They departed again, only to return with a second load of loot and ten or fifteen other women and youths, who were attendants of the two chieftains.

The women and children making up a man's attendants may be compared to a military unit for which he is responsible in various ways, as in matters of instruction, discipline, and support. He also leads them in their unending strife with other communities and with the red Martians. His women are in no sense wives. The green Martians use no word corresponding with this earthly concept. Their mating is a matter of community interest solely, and is directed without reference to natural selection. The council of chieftains of each community control the matter as carefully as the owner of Kentucky racing horses directs the scientific breeding of his stock for the improvement of their offspring.

In theory this may sound acceptable, but the results of this unnatural practice is shown in the cold, cruel creatures, and their gloomy, loveless, joyless existence.

It is true that the green Martians are usually virtuous, both men and women, with the exception of such degenerates as Tal Hajus. But they would be better off with a balance of earthly human characteristics even at the expense of a slight and occasional loss of chastity.

Finding that I must assume responsibility for these creatures, I made the best of it and directed them to find quarters on the upper floors, leaving the third floor to me. I charged one of the girls with the duties of my simple food preparation, and directed the others to take up the various activities they had previously performed. I did not see much of them after that, which is just as well.

CHAPTER 13

Lovemaking on Mars

Following the battle with the airships, the community remained inside the city for several days, abandoning the homeward march until they felt safe that the ships would not return. To be caught on the open plains with a cavalcade of chariots filled with women and children was far from the desire of even the warlike green Martians.

During our period of inactivity, Tars Tarkas instructed me in many of the customs and arts of war used by the Tharks, including lessons in riding the large beasts that carried the warriors. These creatures, known as thoats, are as dangerous and vicious as their masters, but once trained are manageable.

Two of these animals had came to me from the defeated warriors whose metal I now wore, and in a short time I could handle them quite as well as the native warriors. The control method was not at all complicated. If the thoats did not respond with sufficient quickness to the telepathic instructions of their riders, they were struck between the ears with the butt of a pistol. If the creature showed resistance, this treatment was continued until the brute was either under control, or threw off the rider.

If a thoat threw his rider, it became a life and death struggle between the man and the beast. If the rider was quick enough with his pistol he might live to ride again, though on some other beast. If not, his torn and mangled body was gathered up by his women and burned in accordance with Tharkian custom.

My experience with Woola led me to attempt kindness in the treatment of my thoats. First I taught them that they could not unseat me, and even rapped them sharply between the ears to impress them with my authority. Then, by degrees, I won their confidence the same way as I had done countless times with my many horses on Earth. I was good with animals, and I was always kind and humane in my dealings with them. I could take a human life with far less regret than that of a poor, unreasoning, irresponsible animal.

In the course of a few days my thoats were the wonder of the entire community. They would follow me like dogs, rubbing their snouts against my body in awkward evidence of affection, and respond to my every command with a quickness previously unknown on Mars.

"How have you bewitched them?" asked Tars Tarkas one afternoon, after he had seen me put my arm into the mouth of one of my thoats. The poor brute had wedged a piece of stone between two of his teeth while feeding in our courtyard.

"By kindness," I replied. "You see, Tars Tarkas, softer actions have their value, even to a warrior. In the height of battle, as well as on the march, I know that my thoats will obey my every command, and therefore my fighting efficiency is improved. I am a better warrior because I am a kind master. Your other warriors would find it to their advantage to adopt my methods. Why even you, yourself, told me that these wild brutes could occasionally turn victory into defeat when they unseat and attack their riders."

"Show me how you accomplish these results," was Tars Tarkas's only reply.

And so I carefully went through the entire method of training I had adopted with my beasts, and later he had me repeat it for Lorquas Ptomel and some other assembled warriors. That moment marked the beginning of a new existence for our thoats. Before I left the community of Lorquas Ptomel I had the satisfaction of observing a regiment of these highly trained mounts and warriors displaying skills and coordination comparable to what might be seen on an earthly cavalry parade ground. The effect on the precision of the military movements was so remarkable that Lorquas Ptomel presented me with a massive anklet of gold as a sign of his appreciation of my service to the horde.

During the days preceding our departure for the city of Thark, I had seen little of Dejah Thoris. The few times I had visited her quarters she had been absent, walking on the streets with Sola, or investigating the buildings around the plaza. But on the evening before our departure I saw the two of them approaching along one of the avenues. I went to meet them, and taking responsibility for Dejah Thoris's safekeeping, I directed Sola to return to her quarters on some trivial errand. I liked and trusted Sola, but I wanted to be alone with Dejah Thoris. There seemed to be bonds of mutual interest between us as powerful as if we had been born under the same roof rather than on different planets.

I was positive that she shared my feelings in this respect, for on my approach her look of pitiful hopelessness was replaced by a smile of joyful welcome as she placed her hand on my left shoulder in a true red Martian salute.

"Sarkoja told Sola that you had become a true Thark, and that I would now see no more of you than any of the other warriors."

"Sarkoja is a liar of the first magnitude, regardless of the Thark's proud claim of absolute truthfulness."

Dejah Thoris laughed and replied, "I knew that even though you became a member of the community you would not cease to be my friend. 'A warrior may change his metal, but not his heart,' is the saying on Barsoom.

"I think they have been trying to keep us apart," she continued, "for whenever you have been off duty, one of Tars Tarkas's women has always come up with some excuse to get me out of sight. They even have had me down in the pits helping them mix their awful radium powder and make their terrible bullets."

While I was interested in Dejah Thoris's explanation, I was more concerned by their treatment of her. That they were keeping her away from me was not a matter of surprise, but that they would subject her to dangerous labor filled me with rage.

"Have they been mistreating you?" I demanded, feeling the hot blood of my fighting ancestors leap in my veins as I awaited her reply.

"Only in little ways, John Carter," she answered. "Nothing that can harm me outside my pride. They know that I am the daughter of ten thousand jeddaks, that I trace my ancestry straight back without a break to the builder of the first great waterway, and they, who do not even know their own mothers, are jealous of me. At heart they hate their horrible fates, and so inflict their spite on me because I stand for everything they do not have, and for all they most crave and never can attain. Let us pity them, my chieftain, for even though we may die at their hands we are greater than they are and they know it."

Had I known the significance of those words "my chieftain," as applied by a red Martian woman to a man, I would have had the surprise of my life, but I did not know at that time, or for many months thereafter. Yes, I still had much to learn on Barsoom.

"I think it is better that we bow to our fate with as good grace as possible, my princess. But I hope that I am present the next time that any Martian, green, red, pink, or violet, has the nerve to even so much as frown at you," I replied.

Dejah Thoris caught her breath at my last words, and gazed at me with longing eyes and quickening breath, and then, with an odd little laugh, she shook her head and cried, "What a child! A great warrior and yet a stumbling little child."

"What have I done now?" I asked, and hoped my broken heart was not too visible.

"Some day you shall know, John Carter, if we live, but unfortunately, I may not tell you. And remember, I, the daughter of Mors Kajak, son of Tardos Mors, have listened without anger," she stated in conclusion.

Then she broke out again into one of her gay, happy, laughing moods—joking with me on my prowess as a Thark warrior as contrasted with my soft heart and natural kindness.

"I presume that if you accidentally wound an enemy you would take him home and nurse him back to health," she laughed.

"That is precisely what we do on Earth. At least among civilized men."

This made her laugh again. She could not understand it, for with all her tenderness and womanly sweetness, she was still a Martian, and to a Martian the only good enemy is a dead enemy. Every dead adversary means more to divide among those who live.

I was curious to know what I had said or done to cause her so much agitation a moment before and so I again asked her to enlighten me.

"No," she exclaimed, "it is enough that you have said it and that I have listened. And when you learn, John Carter, and if I be dead, as likely I shall be before the farther moon has circled Barsoom another twelve times, remember that I listened and that I . . . smiled."

Day had now given way to night and as we wandered along the avenue lit up by the two moons of Barsoom, and with Earth looking down on us out of her luminous green eye, it seemed that we were alone in the universe, and I, at least, was content.

The chill of the Martian night was upon us, and removing my silks I threw them across her shoulders. As my arm touched her for an instant I felt a thrill pass through every fiber of my being such as contact with no other mortal had ever produced. It seemed that she had leaned slightly toward me, but of that I was not sure. I only knew that as my arm rested there across her shoulders she did not draw away, nor did she speak. And so, in silence, we walked the surface of a dying world, but in my heart had been born that which is ever oldest, yet ever new.

I loved Dejah Thoris . . . the touch of my arm on her naked shoulder had spoken to me in words I could not mistake, and I knew that I had loved her since the first moment my eyes had met hers in the plaza of the dead city of Korad.

A Duel to the Death

My first impulse was to tell her of my love, but then I thought of the helplessness of her position. I knew that I alone could lighten the burdens of her captivity and protect her against the thousands of enemies she must face with our arrival at the city of Thark. I could not chance causing her additional pain by declaring a love which, in all probability she did not return. Should I be so indiscreet, her position would be even more unbearable than now, and the thought that she might feel I was taking advantage of her helplessness to influence her decision was the final argument which sealed my lips.

"Why are you so quiet, Dejah Thoris?" I asked. "Would you like to return to Sola and your quarters?"

"No," she murmured, "I am happy here. I do not know why it is that I should be happy and contented when you are with me. Yet at such times it seems that I am safe and that I shall soon return to my father's court and feel his strong arms around me and my mother's tears and kisses on my cheek."

"Do people kiss, then, on Barsoom?"

"Parents, brothers, and sisters, yes, and," she added in a low, thoughtful tone, "lovers."

"And you, Dejah Thoris, have parents and brothers and sisters?"

"Yes."

"And a—lover?"

She was silent, and I did not attempt to repeat the question.

"The man of Barsoom," she finally ventured, "does not ask personal questions of women, except his mother, and the woman he has fought for and won."

"But I have fought—" I started, and then I wished my tongue had been cut from my mouth for she turned even as I caught myself and ceased speaking. She removed my silks from her shoulder and held them out to me. Without a word, and with her head held high, she moved with the carriage of a queen toward her quarters.

I did not attempt to follow her, other than to see that she reached the building in safety, but directing Woola to accompany her, I turned and entered my own house. I sat for hours meditating on the role chance plays on us poor mortals.

So this was love! I had escaped it for all the years I had roamed the Earth's continents and their encircling seas. In spite of beautiful women and urging opportunity, in spite of a half-desire for love and a constant search for my ideal, it had remained for me to fall furiously and hopelessly in love with a creature from another world, of a species similar, yet not identical with mine. I cared for a woman who was hatched from an egg and whose life span might cover a thousand years! A woman whose people had strange customs and ideas, a woman whose hopes, whose pleasures, whose standards of virtue and of right and wrong might vary as greatly from mine as did those of the green Martians.

Yes, I was a fool, but I was in love, and though I was suffering the greatest misery I had ever known, I would not have had it otherwise for all the riches of Barsoom. Such is love, and such are lovers wherever love is known.

To me, Dejah Thoris was all that was perfect; all that was virtuous and beautiful and noble and good. I believed it then on that night in Korad while the nearer moon of Barsoom raced through the western sky toward the horizon and I believe it today as I sit at my desk in my study overlooking the Hudson River. Twenty years have intervened; for ten of them I lived and fought for Dejah Thoris and her people, and for ten I have lived with her memory.

The morning of our departure for Thark dawned clear and hot, as do all Martian mornings except for the six weeks when the snow melts at the poles. I sought out Dejah Thoris in the throng of departing chariots, but she turned away from me, and I could see the blush rise to her cheek. With the foolish inconsistency of love I held my peace when I might have said something about my ignorance and thus obtained some forgiveness.

My duty dictated that I must see that she was comfortable, and so I glanced into her chariot and rearranged her silks and furs. In doing so I noted with horror that she was heavily chained by one ankle to the side of the vehicle.

"What does this mean?" I cried, turning to Sola.

"Sarkoja thought it best," she answered, her face showing her disapproval of the procedure.

Examining the manacles, I saw that they fastened with a massive spring lock.

"Where is the key, Sola? Let me have it."

"Sarkoja wears it, John Carter," she answered.

I turned without further word and sought out Tars Tarkas, and strongly objected to the unnecessary humiliations and cruelties that were being heaped upon Dejah Thoris.

"John Carter, if you and Dejah Thoris are to escape the Tharks it will be on this journey. We know that you will not go without her. You have shown yourself a mighty fighter, and we do not wish to manacle you, so we hold you both in the easiest way that will ensure security. I have spoken."

I saw the strength of his reasoning at a flash, and knew that I should not appeal his decision, but I asked that the key be taken from Sarkoja and that she be directed to leave the prisoner alone.

"This much, Tars Tarkas, you may do for me in return for the friendship that I feel for you."

"Friendship?" he replied. "There is no such thing, John Carter; but you may have your will. I shall direct that Sarkoja cease to annoy the girl, and I myself will take custody of the key."

"Unless you wish me to assume the responsibility," I said, smiling.

He looked at me long and earnestly before he spoke.

"If you were to give me your word that neither you nor Dejah Thoris would attempt to escape until after we have safely reached the court of Tal Hajus, I would give you the key and throw the chains into the River Iss."

"It would be better that you hold the key, Tars Tarkas," I replied.

He smiled and said no more, but that night as we were making camp I saw him unfasten Dejah Thoris's fetters himself.

With all his cruel ferocity and coldness there was an undercurrent of something in Tars Tarkas which he seemed battling to control. Could it be a part of some human instinct from an ancient ancestor haunting him with the horror of his people's ways?

As I was approaching Dejah Thoris's chariot I passed Sarkoja, and the black, poisonous look she gave me was the sweetest balm I had felt for many hours. Lord, how she hated me! It bristled from her so much that one might almost cut it with a sword.

A few moments later I saw her deep in conversation with a warrior named Zad; a big, hulking, powerful brute, but one who had never made a kill among his own chieftains. As Sarkoja talked with Zad, he cast occasional glances in my direction, while she seemed to be urging him to some action. I paid little attention to it at the time, but the next day I had good reason to recall these circumstances. I also gained insight into the depths of Sarkoja's hatred and how far she would go to achieve her vengeance.

Dejah Thoris would have nothing to do with me again this evening, and though I spoke her name she neither replied, nor conceded by so much as the flutter of an eyelid that she recognized my existence. In my pain, I did what most other lovers would have done; I sought word of her through an intimate—I intercepted Sola in another part of camp.

"What is the matter with Dejah Thoris?" I blurted out. "Why won't she speak to me?"

Sola, herself, seemed puzzled—like such strange actions on the part of two humans were beyond her understanding.

"She says you have angered her, and that is all she will say, except that she is the daughter of a jed and the granddaughter of a jeddak and she has been humiliated by a creature who is not fit to clean the teeth of her grandmother's sorak."

I pondered over this report for some time, finally asking, "And just what is a 'sorak'?"

"A little animal about as big as my hand, which the red Martian women keep as a pet," she explained.

Not fit to polish the teeth of her grandmother's cat! I must rank pretty low in the consideration of Dejah Thoris, but I could not help laughing at the strange figure of speech, so homely and so earthly. It made me homesick . . . it sounded so much like "not fit to polish her shoes."

We broke camp the next day at an early hour and marched until around noon when we halted to rest the animals. I was changing riding cloths from one of my thoats to the other, when Zad approached me and, without a word, struck my animal a terrific blow with the flat of his sword!

I did not need a manual of green Martian manners to know how to reply to this hostile act.

In fact, I was so wild with anger that I could scarcely keep from drawing my pistol and shooting him down for the brute he was; but he stood waiting with drawn sword, and my only choice was to draw my own and meet him in a fair fight.

I knew he prided himself on his ability with the sword but I was ready to match him with his choice of weapon. The fight that followed was a long one and delayed the resumption of the march for an hour. The entire community surrounded us, leaving a clear space about one hundred feet in diameter for our battle.

Zad first attempted to rush me like a bull might charge a wolf, but I was much too quick for him. Each time I sidestepped his rush he would go lunging past me, only to receive a nick from my sword on his arm or back. He was soon streaming blood from a half dozen minor wounds, but I could not get an opening to deliver an effective thrust. Then he changed his tactics, and fighting warily and with extreme dexterity, he tried to do by science what he was unable to do by brute strength. I must admit that he was a magnificent swordsman, and if it had not been for my greater endurance and the remarkable agility the lesser gravitation of Mars gave me, I might not have been able to put up the fight I did against him.

We circled for some time without doing much damage on either side. The long, straight, needle-like swords flashed in the sunlight, and rang out in the stillness as they crashed together with each parry. Finally Zad, realizing that he was tiring more than I, decided to close in and end the battle in a final blaze of glory. But just as he rushed me, a blinding flash of light struck my eyes so that I could not see his approach! I could only leap blindly to one side in an effort to escape the deadly blade and it seemed like I could already feel it slice into my vitals. I knew my evasion was only partially successful, as I felt a sharp pain in my left shoulder, but in the sweep of my glance as I sought to locate my adversary, a sight met my astonished gaze that paid me well for the wound. There, upon Dejah Thoris's chariot stood three figures, Dejah Thoris, Sola, and Sarkoja, and as my fleeting glance swept over them I viewed a drama that will stand carved in my memory to the day of my death.

As I looked, Dejah Thoris turned on Sarkoja with the fury of a young tigress and struck something from her upraised hand; something that flashed in the sunlight as it spun to the ground. Then I knew what had blinded me at that crucial moment of the fight, and how Sarkoja had found a way to kill me without delivering the final thrust herself.

And I saw another thing that almost cost me my life then and there. It took my mind from my opponent for an instant as I watched Dejah

Thoris strike the tiny mirror from Sarkoja's hand and Sarkoja, her face livid with hatred and rage, whipped out her dagger and stabbed at Dejah Thoris. But then Sola, our dear and faithful Sola, jumped between them and the last I saw was the dagger descending.

My enemy recovered from his last thrust and was making it extremely interesting for me, so I reluctantly turned my attention to the work at hand, but my mind was not on the battle.

We rushed each other furiously time after time, until suddenly, feeling the sharp point of his sword at my chest in a thrust I could neither parry nor escape, I threw myself on him with outstretched sword and, with all the weight of my body, decided that I would not die alone if I could prevent it. I felt his steel tear into my chest, all went black, my head whirled in dizziness, and I felt my knees giving out beneath me.

ade a most imposing and awe-inspiring
as we strung out across the yellow land-
e two hundred and fifty ornate and
olored chariots, preceded by an advance
some two hundred mounted warriors
ains riding five abreast and followed by
ber in the same formation, with a score
f flankers on either side. There were fifty
todons, the heavy draft animals known
, and about five hundred of the warriors'
ts running loose within a hollow square
y some following warriors. The green
leaming metal ornaments and jewels,
. in the trappings of the zitidars and
d interspersed with the flashing colors of
t silks and furs and feathers, lent a bar-
dor to the caravan which would have
East Indian prince green with envy.

normous broad tires of the chariots and
d feet of the animals made no sound on
covered sea bottom and we moved in
ce, except when the stillness was bro-
 growling of a complaining zitidar, or
ling of fighting thoats. The green
lid not converse much, and then usual-
osyllables, low and like the faint rum-
stant thunder.

veled over a trackless waste of moss,
ding to the pressure of broad tire or
t, rose up again behind us, leaving no

CHAPTER 15

Sola Tells Me Her Story

When consciousness returned—and as I soon learned, I was down but a moment—I sprang quickly to my feet searching for my sword. I found it, buried to the hilt in Zad's green chest, as he lay stone dead on the ground. I regained my full senses and found his weapon piercing my chest and coming out below the shoulder. As I lunged I had turned so that his sword merely inflicted a painful but not dangerous wound.

Removing his blade from my body I also retrieved my own, and turning my back to his ugly carcass, I moved, sick, sore, stabbed and disgusted, toward the chariots that held my attendants and my belongings. A murmur of Martian applause greeted me, but I hardly noticed it.

Bleeding and weak I reached my women, who, accustomed to such happenings, dressed my wounds, applying the wonderful Martian healing potions. Give a Martian woman a chance and death must take a back seat. They soon had me patched up so that, except for weakness from loss of blood and a little soreness around the wound, I suffered no great distress from this thrust which, under normal earthly treatment, would have put me flat on my back for days.

As soon as they were through with me I hastened to the chariot of Dejah Thoris, where I found my poor Sola with her chest also covered with bandages, but apparently little the worse for her encounter with Sarkoja. The dagger had struck the edge of one of Sola's metal ornaments and, thus deflected, inflicted only a slight flesh wound.

As I approached, I found Dejah Thoris lying prone on her silks and furs, her lovely form wracked with sobs. She did not notice my presence, nor did she hear me speaking with Sola, standing a short distance away.

"Is she injured?" I asked Sola, indicating Dejah Thoris by a nod of my head.

"No, but she thinks that you are dead."

"And that her grandmother's cat may now have no one to clean its teeth?" I asked, smiling.

"John Carter, I do not understand either her ways or yours, but I am sure the granddaughter of ten thousand jeddaks would never mourn like this over anyone unless they held the highest claim upon her affections. They are a proud race,

but they are just, as are
must have wronged her
erate your existence li
when she thinks you de

"Tears are a strang
she continued, "and so
interpret them. Other t
only seen but two peopl
wept from sorrow, the
The first was my mothe
killed her; the other
dragged her from me to

"Your mother!" I ex
could not have known y

"But I did. And I kr
you would like to hea
Barsoomian story, come
John Carter, and I will
have never spoken in all
the signal has been given
you must go."

"I will come tonight
sure to tell Dejah Thoris
not force myself upon h
do not let her know I sav
speak with me I but awai

Sola mounted the ch
ing into its place in line, a
ing thoat and galloped to
Tarkas.

We
spectacl
scape.
brightly
guard o
and chi
a like n
or more
extra n
as zitid
extra th
formed
horde'
duplica
thoats,
magni
baric s
turnec

Th
the pa
the m
utter
ken b
the s
Mart
ly in
bling

V
whic
padd

sign that we had passed. We might have been the ghosts of the departed dead upon the dead sea of that dying planet for all the sound or sign we made in passing. It was the first march of a large body of men and animals I had ever witnessed that raised no dust and left no spoor; for there is no dust on Mars except in the cultivated districts during the winter months, and even then the absence of high winds renders it almost unnoticeable.

We camped that night at the foot of the hills marking the southern boundary of this particular sea. Our animals had been two days without drink, but as Tars Tarkas explained to me, they require little water and can live almost indefinitely on the moss that covers Barsoom, and holds in its tiny stems sufficient moisture to meet the limited demands of the animals. After my evening meal I looked for Sola and found her working by the light of a torch on some of Tars Tarkas's equipment. She looked up at my approach, her face beaming with pleasure and welcome.

"I am glad you came," she said; "Dejah Thoris sleeps and I am lonely. My own people do not care for me, John Carter; I am too unlike them. It is a sad fate, since I must live my life among them, and I often wish that I were a true green Martian woman, without love and without hope; but I have known love and so I am lost.

"I promised to tell you my story, or rather the story of my parents. From what I have learned of you and the ways of your people I am sure that the tale will not seem strange to you, but among green Martians it has no parallel within the memory of the oldest living Thark.

"My mother was rather small, in fact too small to be allowed the responsibilities of maternity, as our chieftains breed mainly for size. She was also less cold and cruel than most green Martian women, and caring little for their society, she often roamed the deserted avenues in the city alone. Sometimes she went and sat among the wild flowers that cover the nearby hills, thinking thoughts and wishing wishes which I alone among Tharkian women today could understand, for am I not the child of my mother?

"And there among the hills she met a young warrior guarding the grazing zitidars and thoats. The two spoke at first only of such things as might be of interest in a community of Tharks, but gradually, as they came to meet more often— and no longer by chance—they talked about themselves, their likes, their ambitions and their hopes. She trusted him and told him of the distaste she felt for the cruelties of their people, for the hideous, loveless lives they must lead. She then waited for a storm of abuse to break from his cold, hard lips; but instead he took her in his arms and kissed her.

"They kept their love a secret for six long years. My mother was an attendant to the great

Tal Hajus, while her lover was a simple warrior, wearing only his own metal. If their defection from Tharkian traditions had been discovered, both would have paid the penalty with their blood in the great arena in front of Tal Hajus and the assembled hordes.

"The egg from which I came was hidden beneath a glass vessel on the highest and most inaccessible tower of ancient Thark. Once each year my mother visited it as it lay there in the process of incubation. She dared not come more frequently, for she feared that her every move was being watched. During this period my father gained great distinction as a warrior and had taken the metal from several chieftains. His love for my mother never stopped, and his ambition in life was to reach a point where he could fight Tal Hajus and take his metal. Thus, as ruler of the Tharks, he would be free to claim my mother as his own, as well as protect their child.

"It was a wild dream—that my father might win Tal Hajus's metal in five short years—but his advance was rapid, and he soon stood high in the councils of Thark. But one day the chance was lost forever as he was ordered away to the ice-clad south to make war with the southern natives.

"He was gone four years, and when he returned all had been over for three. The forbidden egg hatched about a year after his departure and just before the return of an expedition sent out to fetch the fruits of our community incubator. My mother continued to keep me in the old tower, visiting me nightly and showering me with the love the community life would have robbed from us both. She hoped to mix me in with the other new hatchlings and escape the fate that would surely follow the discovery of her sin against the traditions of the green men.

"She quickly taught me the language and customs of my kind, and one night she told me the story I have told to you up to this point, impressing me with the need for secrecy. She told me I must exercise caution after she placed me with the other young Tharks. I was not to show that I was further advanced in education and to never divulge in the presence of others my affection for her. And finally, she drew me close and whispered the name of my father.

"And then a light flashed out in the darkness of the tower chamber, and there stood Sarkoja, her gleaming eyes fixed in a frenzy of loathing and contempt on my mother! The torrent of hatred and abuse she poured out turned my young heart cold in terror. She had long suspected something because of my mother's nightly absences from her quarters and now Sarkoja knew the story.

"The one thing she had not heard was the whispered name of my father. This was apparent from her repeated demands for my mother to disclose the name of her partner in sin. To save me from torture she lied and told Sarkoja that she alone knew the father's name.

"Sarkoja ran to Tal Hajus to reported her discovery. When she was gone my mother, carrying me wrapped in silks and furs, went down to the streets and ran wildly away toward the southern outskirts of the city. As we neared the border a sound came to us from across the mossy flat leading to the gates. The sounds we heard were the squealing of thoats and the grumbling of zitidars, with the occasional clank of arms that announced the approach of a body of warriors. Uppermost in my mother's mind was the hope that it was my father returning from his expedition.

"Retreating into the shadows of a doorway she awaited the coming of the cavalcade that shortly entered the avenue, breaking its formation and thronging the thoroughfare from wall to wall. As the head of the procession passed, the lesser moon swung clear of the overhanging roofs and lit up the scene with all the brilliancy of her wondrous light. My mother shrank back into the shadows, and from her hiding place saw that the expedition was not my father's, but the returning caravan bearing the young, freshly hatched Tharks. Instantly she formed a plan, and as a chariot swung close to our hiding place she slipped quietly onboard, crouching low in the shadow of the high side, hugging me tightly in a frenzy of love.

"She knew that never again would she hold me, nor was it likely we would ever look upon each other again. In the confusion of the plaza she mixed me in with the other children, whose guardians during the journey were now free to relinquish their responsibility. We were herded together into a large room, fed by women who had not accompanied the expedition, and the next day we were parceled out among the chieftains.

"I never saw my mother again after that night. She was imprisoned by Tal Hajus, and every effort, including the most horrible and shameful torture, was brought to bear to wring from her lips the name of my father. But she remained steadfast and loyal, dying at last amidst the laughter of Tal Hajus and his chieftains.

"I learned afterward that she told them that she had killed me to save me from a similar fate at their hands, and that she had thrown my body to the white apes. Sarkoja did not believe her, and I feel to this day that she suspects my true origin, but does not dare expose me, because she also guesses the identity of my father.

"I was present when he returned from his expedition and learned the story of my mother's fate from Tal Hajus. From that moment on my father was the cruelest of the cruel, and I am waiting for the day when he shall win the goal of his ambition, and feel the carcass of Tal Hajus beneath his foot. I am sure that he waits for an opportunity to wreak a terrible vengeance on Tal Hajus and that his love is as strong now as when it blossomed nearly forty years ago. I am sure of these facts as I am that we sit here at the edge of an ancient dried up ocean while sensible people sleep."

"And your father, Sola, is he here in camp with us now?"

"Yes, but he does not know me for what I am, nor does he know who betrayed my mother to Tal Hajus. I alone know my father's name, and only I and Tal Hajus and Sarkoja know that it was she who carried the tale that brought death and torture to the woman he loved."

We sat silent for a few moments, she, wrapped in the gloomy thoughts of her terrible past, and I in pity for the poor creatures whom the heartless, senseless customs of their race had doomed to loveless lives of cruelty and hate. Finally she spoke, "John Carter, I know that I can trust you, and because this knowledge may someday help you, I am going to tell you the name of my father. When the time comes, speak the truth if it seems best to you. I trust you because I know that you are not cursed with the terrible trait of absolute and unswerving truthfulness, that you could lie if a lie would save others from sorrow or suffering. My father's name is . . . Tars Tarkas."

We Plan Escape

The rest of our journey to the city of Thark was uneventful. We were on the road twenty days, crossing two sea bottoms and passing through a number of ruined cities, mostly smaller than Korad. Twice we crossed the famous Martian waterways, or canals, so-called by our earthly astronomers.

Crossing in the darkness, I was not able to see much, except when the nearer moon, in her wild and ceaseless hurtling through the Barsoomian heavens, lit up patches of the landscape, disclosing walled fields and low, rambling buildings, looking much like farms on my home planet. There were animals in a few of the enclosures, and they announced our presence by their loud squealing and snorting as soon as they scented our strange wild beasts and wilder green men.

Only once did I see someone—the fellow must have been sleeping beside the road—for as we came up to him, he got up and, after a single glance at the approaching caravan, fled madly down the road, scaling a nearby wall with the agility of a cat. The Tharks ignored him since they were not on the warpath, and the only sign that they had seen him was a quickening of our pace toward the desert.

Not once did I talk with Dejah Thoris. She sent no word to me that I would be welcome at her chariot, and my foolish pride kept me from making any advances. I believe that a man's way with women is in inverse ratio to his prowess among men. Weaker men often have great ability to charm the fair sex, while the fighting man, who can face a thousand real dangers, sits like some frightened child when he is in the presence of a lady.

Just thirty days after my arrival on Barsoom we entered the ancient city of Thark, from whose long-forgotten people these green men must have stolen their name. The hordes of Thark number some thirty thousand souls, and are divided into twenty-five communities. Each community has its own jed and lesser chieftains, but all are under the rule of Tal Hajus, Jeddak of Thark.

We made our entry into the great central plaza early in the afternoon. There were no enthusiastic friendly greetings. Those who chanced to be in sight spoke the names of warriors or women with whom they came in direct contact, in the formal subdued greeting of their kind. When it was discovered that the new arrivals brought two captives, they showed a greater interest, and Dejah Thoris and I were the centers of noisy, inquiring groups.

We were soon assigned to quarters, and the balance of the day was devoted to getting settled. The same grand architecture I had seen in other cities was in evidence here, only on an even larger and richer scale. My quarters would have been suitable for housing Earth's greatest emperors.

When my house was finally put in order, it was nearing sunset, and I went out with the intention of locating Sola and her charges. I wanted to talk with Dejah Thoris and form a truce until I could find some way to make our escape. I finally spotted the ugly head of Woola peering from a second-story window. Without waiting for an invitation I bolted up the winding runway and was greeted by the frenzied animal who threw his great carcass at me, nearly knocking me on the floor. The poor old fellow was so glad to see me that I thought he would devour me, his head split from ear to ear, showing his three rows of tusks in his monstrous smile.

Quieting him with a word of command, I looked through the approaching gloom for a sign of Dejah Thoris, and then, not seeing her, I called her name. There was an answering murmur from the far corner of the apartment, and with a couple of quick strides I stood next to her where she sat among the furs and silks on an ancient carved wooden seat. As I waited, she rose to her full height and said: "What would John Carter desire of his captive?"

"Dejah Thoris, I do not know how I have angered you. It was never my desire to hurt or offend you—I hoped only to protect and comfort you. Have none of me if it is your will, but you must aid me in making your escape. This is not a request, but my command. When you are safe once more at your father's court you may do with me as you please, but from now until that day I am your master, and you must obey and aid me."

She looked at me long and earnestly and I thought that she was softening toward me. "I understand your words, John Carter, but it is you, yourself, I do not understand. You are a strange mixture of child and man, of brute and noble. I only wish that I might read your heart."

"Look down at your feet, dearest lady. My heart lies there where it has been since that other night at Korad, and where it will always lie, beating alone for you, until death stills it forever."

She took a little step toward me, her beautiful hands outstretched in a strange, groping gesture.

"What do you mean?" she whispered. "What are you saying to me?"

"I am saying the words I promised myself that I would not say to you, at least until you were no longer a captive among the green men. I am saying that I am yours, body and soul, to serve you, to fight for you, and to die for you. Whatever I may do for you will be prompted solely from my selfish motives, since it gives me more pleasure to serve you than not."

"I will respect your wishes, John Carter, because I understand the motives that prompt them. I accept your service no more willingly than I bow to your authority but your word shall be my law. I have twice wronged you in my thoughts and again I ask your forgiveness."

Further conversation was prevented by the entrance of a very agitated Sola, who cried, "That horrible Sarkoja has been to see Tal Hajus, and from what I heard out on the plaza there is little hope for either of you!"

"What do they say?" demanded Dejah Thoris.

"That you will be thrown to the wild calots in the great arena as soon as the hordes have assembled for the yearly games!"

"Sola," I said, "you are a Thark, but you hate and loathe the customs of your people as much as we do. Will you come with us when we try to escape? I'm sure that Dejah Thoris can offer you a home and protection among her people, and your fate could be no worse there among them than it would be here."

"Yes," cried Dejah Thoris, "come with us, Sola! You will be better off among the red men of Helium than you are here, and I can promise you not only a home with us, but the love and affection your nature craves and that would always be denied you by the customs of your own race. Come with us, Sola . . . we could go without you, but your fate would be terrible if they thought you helped us to leave. I know that you would not interfere with our escape, but we want you with us, we want you to come to a land of sunshine and happiness, among a people who know the meaning of love, sympathy, and gratitude. Say that you will, Sola! Tell me that you will come with us!"

"The great waterway leading to Helium is but fifty miles to the south," murmured Sola, half to herself. "A swift thoat might make it in three hours; and then to Helium it is five hundred miles, most of the way through thinly settled districts. My people would follow us. We might hide among the great trees for a time, but the chances of escape are small indeed. They would follow us to the very gates of Helium."

"Is there no other way we might reach Helium?" I asked. "Can you draw me a map of the country we must travel, Dejah Thoris?"

She nodded, and taking a large diamond from her hair drew on the marble floor the first map of Barsoomian territory I had ever seen. It was crisscrossed in every direction with long straight lines, sometimes running parallel and sometimes converging toward a circle. The lines, she said, were waterways; the circles, cities; and one far to the northwest she pointed out as Helium. There were other cities closer, but she said she feared to enter many of them, because they were not all friendly toward Helium.

Finally, after studying the map carefully, I pointed out a waterway far to the north that also seemed to lead to Helium and asked, "Does this go through your grandfather's territory?"

"Yes, but it is two hundred miles north of us; it is one of the waterways we crossed on the trip to Thark."

"They would never suspect we would try for that distant waterway," I answered, "it is the best route for our escape."

Sola agreed with me, and we all decided to leave the city that very night—just as quickly as I could saddle my thoats. Leaving the females to gather what food, silks, and furs we were to need, I slipped quietly to the first floor and entered the courtyard where our animals were confined.

Beneath the radiance of the Martian moons moved the herd of thoats and zitidars. As they scented me they became more restless. It was risky business, entering the corral alone and at night; first, because the noise might warn nearby warriors that something was amiss, and also because some thoat might charge me.

Having no desire to awaken any nasty tempers on such a night as this, I hugged the shadows of the buildings, ready to leap into the safety of a nearby doorway. I moved silently to the gates and called softly to my two animals. I was pleased that my prior horse training experience on Earth, applied to these Martian brutes, allowed me to win their love and confidence, for soon, from the far side of the court, I saw their two huge bulks forcing their way toward me.

They came to me, rubbing their muzzles against my body and sniffing around for the bits of food I always kept for their treats. After leading the animals out and closing the gate, I walked them quietly toward a deserted avenue that led toward the point where I had arranged to meet Dejah Thoris and Sola. With the noiselessness of disembodied spirits we moved along the deserted streets, but not until we were within sight of the plain beyond the city did I start to breathe freely.

I reached our meeting place safely, but since they were not there I led my animals into the entrance hall of one of the large buildings. I did not feel any undue apprehension until nearly an hour passed. By the time another half hour had crawled away I was becoming filled with grave anxiety. Then the stillness of the night was broken by the sound of an approaching party and from the black shadows of my entranceway I saw a score of mounted warriors and heard words that almost made my heart jump out of my chest.

"He likely arranged to meet them just outside the city, and so—" I heard no more, they had passed on; but it was enough. Our plan had been discovered, and the chances for escape now would be small indeed. My one hope was to return and learn what fate had overtaken Dejah Thoris, but how to do it with these monstrous thoats on my hands was a big problem.

Suddenly an idea occurred to me, and acting on my knowledge of the construction of these Martian buildings with their large court in the center of each square, I groped my way blindly through the dark chambers, calling the thoats after me. We finally got to the inner court where they would be quiet and content and there was only the remotest possibility that they would be discovered. The green men had no desire to enter these outlying buildings, frequented by the only thing that caused them fear—the great white apes of Barsoom.

Turning the beasts loose, I quickly made my way outside. Waiting in the doorway until I was sure no one was near, I hurried across the street and through the first doorway to the court beyond. I repeated this technique, crossing through court after court until I made my way to the courtyard in the rear of the quarters that housed Dejah Thoris. I took advantage of my relatively great strength and agility and sprang upward until I grasped the sill of a second-story window. Drawing myself inside I moved toward the front of the building, and not until I had reached the doorway of her room did I hear voices.

I paused and listened, for the conversation I heard was in the low gutturals of men, and the words that finally came to me proved a most timely warning. The speaker was a chieftain and he was giving orders to four of his warriors.

"And when he returns to this chamber," he was saying, "—you four are to capture and disarm him. It will require the combined strength of all of you to do it if the reports they bring back from Korad are correct. Drag him to the vaults beneath the jeddak's quarters and chain him securely until Tal Hajus wishes to see him. There will be no danger of the girl returning, for by this time she is safe in the arms of Tal Hajus, and may all her ancestors have pity; the great Sarkoja has done a noble night's work. I go, and if you fail to capture him, I will send your carcasses to the cold waters of the River Iss."

CHAPTER 17

A Costly Recapture

As the officer stopped speaking, he turned to leave the apartment by the door where I was standing. I had heard enough to fill my soul with dread, and stealing quietly away I returned to the street. My plan of action was instantly formed and I soon stood within the Jeddak of Thark's courtyard.

The brilliantly lit apartments of the first floor told me where to look first. I soon discovered that my entry was not to be the easy thing I had hoped, for the rear rooms bordering the court were filled with warriors and women. I then glanced at the floors above, discovering that the third was unlighted, and soon I had drawn myself within its sheltering shadows.

Fortunately, the room I had selected was unoccupied, and creeping to the corridor I discovered a dim light in the apartments ahead of me. Reaching what appeared to be a doorway I discovered that it was an opening upon an immense inner chamber that rose from the first floor, two stories below me, to the dome-like roof of the building high above my head. The floor of this great circular hall was thronged with chieftains, warriors, and women, and on one side was a platform upon which squatted the most hideous beast I had ever seen. He had all the cold, hard, cruel, terrible features of the green warriors, but there was not a mark of dignity or pride on his bestial countenance, while his enormous bulk spread itself out on the platform where he squatted.

But the sight that froze me was seeing Sola and Dejah Thoris standing there in front of him, and his fiendish leer as he let his great protruding eyes gloat up and down the lines of my love's beautiful figure. She was speaking, but I could not hear what she said, nor could I make out the low grumbling of his reply. She stood there with her head held high, and even I, from across the room, could read the scorn and disgust on her face as she fearlessly glared at him. She was indeed the proud daughter of a thousand jeddaks—so small, so frail beside the towering warriors around her—but in her majesty, dwarfing them into insignificance. She was the mightiest figure among them and I truly believe that they felt it.

Presently Tal Hajus made a sign that the chamber be cleared, and that the prisoners be left alone with him. Slowly the chieftains, the warriors, and the women melted away into the shadows of the surrounding rooms, and Dejah Thoris and Sola stood alone before the Jeddak of the Tharks.

Only one chieftain hesitated before departing; I saw him standing in the shadows of a column, his fingers nervously grasping the hilt of his sword and his cruel eyes aimed in hatred at Tal Hajus. It was Tars Tarkas, and I could read his thoughts like they were an open book with the undisguised loathing on his face. He was thinking of that other woman who, forty years ago, had stood before this beast. If I could have spoken a word into his ear at that moment, the reign of Tal Hajus would have been over. But finally he strode from the room, not knowing he left his own daughter at the mercy of the creature he most detested.

Tal Hajus arose, and I, half fearing, half anticipating his intentions, hurried to the winding runway that led to the floors below. No one was near to intercept me, and I reached the main floor of the chamber unobserved, taking my station in the shadow of the same column that Tars Tarkas had just deserted. As I reached the floor Tal Hajus was speaking.

"Princess of Helium, I might wring a mighty ransom from your people if I would but return you to them unharmed, but I would a thousand times rather watch your beautiful face in the agony of torture; it shall be long and drawn out, that I promise you. Ten days of pleasure for me and ten days of pain for you would be all too short to show the hatred I harbor for your race. The terrors of your death shall haunt the slumbers of the red men through all the ages to come; they will shudder in the shadows of the night as their fathers tell them of the awful vengeance of the green men; of the power and might and cruelty of Tal Hajus. But before the torture you shall be mine for one short night, and word of that too shall go forth to Tardos Mors, Jeddak of Helium, and you can be sure that he will grovel on the ground in the agony of his sorrow. Tomorrow the torture will commence! Tonight you are mine! Come!"

He sprang down from the platform and grasped her roughly by the arm, but barely had he touched her when I leaped between them— my sword, sharp and gleaming in my right hand! I could have plunged it into his putrid heart before he realized anything but as I drew back my arm to strike I thought of Tars Tarkas. With all my rage—with all my hatred—I could not rob him of that sweet moment for which he had lived and hoped all these long, weary years, and so instead, I swung my fist into the tyrant's jaw! Without a sound he slipped to the floor.

In the same deathly silence I grasped Dejah Thoris by the hand, and motioning Sola to follow, we sped noiselessly from the chamber to the floor above. Unseen, we reached a rear window where I lowered, first Sola and then Dejah Thoris, to the ground below. Dropping lightly after them I led the way over the same course I had so recently followed from the distant boundary of the city.

We finally came to my thoats and after saddling them up we quickly wound our way through the building to the avenue beyond. Mounting Sola on one beast, and Dejah Thoris behind me on the other, we rode from the city of Thark. We turned to the northeast and struck out on the mossy waste toward the waterway leading to Helium, two hundred dangerous and weary miles away.

No word was spoken until we had left the city far behind, but I could hear the quiet sobbing of Dejah Thoris as she clung to me with her head resting against my shoulder.

"If we make it, my chieftain, the debt of Helium will be a mighty one; greater than she can ever pay you; and should we not make it the debt is no less, though Helium will never know, for you have saved the last of our line from a fate worse than death."

I did not answer, but instead reached to my side and gently held the hand of the woman I loved where it clung to me for support, and then, in unbroken silence, we sped over the yellow, moonlit moss; each of us occupied with our own thoughts. For my part, I could not be happier if I tried—with the warm body of Dejah Thoris pressed close to mine, and with all our future danger—my heart was singing as gaily as though we were already entering the gates of Helium.

We rode all night and all the following day with only a few short rests. On the second night we were completely exhausted, and so we lay down on the moss and slept for some five or six hours, taking up the journey once more before daylight. All the following day we rode, and when late in the afternoon we had seen no distant trees, the mark of the great waterways throughout all Barsoom, the terrible truth flashed upon us—we were lost.

Evidently we had gotten off course, but which way it was difficult to say. At any rate, no waterway was in sight, and the entire party was almost ready to drop from hunger, thirst and fatigue. Far ahead of us we could distinguish the outlines of low mountains. We decided to attempt to reach them in the hope that from some ridge we might locate the missing waterway. Night fell before we reached our goal, and almost fainting from weakness, we lay down and slept.

I was awakened early in the morning by some huge body pressing close to mine, and opening my eyes with a start, I beheld my blessed Woola snuggling close! The faithful brute had followed us across that trackless waste to share our fate, whatever it might be. Putting my arms around his neck I pressed my cheek close—I am not ashamed of the tears that came to my eyes as I thought of his love for me. Shortly after this Dejah Thoris and Sola woke up, and we pushed on at once in an effort to get to the hills.

We were within a mile of our goal when Dejah Thoris cried out that she saw a party of mounted men filing down from a pass in the hills several miles away. Sola and I both looked in the direction she indicated, and there, plainly as day, were several hundred mounted warriors. They seemed to be headed in a southwesterly direction that would take them away from us.

They probably were Thark warriors who had been sent out to capture us, and we breathed a sigh of relief that they were traveling in the opposite direction. Quickly lifting Dejah Thoris down, I commanded the animals to lie down and we three did the same, presenting as small a viewable object as possible for fear of attracting the attention of the warriors.

We could see them as they filed out of the pass before they were lost to view behind a ridge; if they had been in view for any great length of time, they could hardly have failed to discover us. As the last warrior came into view, he halted, brought his powerful field-glass to his eye and scanned the sea bottom in all directions. As his glass swung toward us I could feel the cold sweat flow from every pore in my body.

Presently the glass came to us and—stopped. The tension on our nerves was near the breaking point, and I doubt if any of us breathed for the few moments he held us covered by his glass; and then he lowered it and we could see him shout a command to the warriors who had passed from our sight behind the ridge. He did not wait for them to join him, as he turned his thoat and came tearing madly in our direction.

There was but one slight chance and that we must take quickly. Raising my strange Martian rifle to my shoulder, I sighted and touched the trigger button; there was a sharp explosion and as the missile reached its goal the charging warrior was knocked off his mount.

Springing to my feet, I urged one thoat to rise, and directed Sola to take Dejah Thoris and make an effort to reach the hills before the green warriors were on us. I knew that in the ravines and gullies they might find a temporary hiding place, and even if they died there of hunger and thirst it would be better than if they fell into the hands of the Tharks. Forcing them to take my two revolvers as a slight means of protection, and as an escape for themselves from the horrid death which recapture would surely mean, I lifted

Dejah Thoris in my arms and threw her up on the thoat behind Sola.

"Goodbye, my princess," I whispered, "we may yet meet in Helium. I have escaped from worse plights than this," and I tried to smile.

"What? Are you not coming with us?"

"How could I, Darling? Someone must hold these fellows off for a while, and I can better escape them alone than I could with the three of us together."

She sprang quickly from the thoat and, throwing her arms about my neck, turned to Sola, saying with quiet dignity: "Fly, Sola! Dejah Thoris remains to die with the man she loves."

Those words are engraved in my heart. Ah, gladly would I give up my life a thousand times if I could only hear them once again; but I could not then spare even a second to the rapture of her sweet embrace, and pressing my lips to hers, I picked her up and again tossed her behind Sola. Commanding Sola to hold her there by force, and then slapping the thoat on the flank, I saw them gallop away; Dejah Thoris struggling to free herself from Sola's grasp.

Turning, I saw the green warriors mounting the ridge and looking for their chieftain. In a moment they saw him . . . and then me. I commenced firing, lying flat on my belly in the moss. I had a hundred rounds in the magazine of my rifle, and another hundred in the belt at my back, and I kept up a continuous stream of fire.

My respite was short-lived however, for soon the entire party, numbering some thousand men, came charging into view, racing madly toward me. I fired until my rifle was empty and they were almost on me. A glance showed me that Dejah Thoris and Sola had disappeared among the hills, so I jumped up, throwing down my useless gun, and started away on foot in the opposite direction.

If ever Martians had an exhibition of jumping, it was granted to those astonished warriors, but while it led them away from Dejah Thoris, it did not distract their attention from my capture.

They chased me until, finally, my foot struck a projecting piece of quartz, and down I went, sprawling on the moss. As I looked up they were on me, and although I drew my sword in an attempt to sell my life as dearly as possible, it was soon over. I reeled beneath their blows falling on me in torrents! My head swam; all was black, and I went down to oblivion.

Chained in Warhoon

It must have been several hours before I regained consciousness and I well remember the feeling of surprise as I realized that I was not dead. I was lying among a pile of sleeping silks and furs and bending over me was an ancient and ugly female. As I opened my eyes, she turned to one of the several green warriors in the room, saying, "He will live, O Jed."

"'Tis well," replied the one so addressed, rising and approaching my couch, "he will show us rare sport at the Great Games!"

And now as my eyes fell upon him, I saw that he was not a Thark, for his ornaments and metal were not of that horde. He was a huge fellow, terribly scarred about the face and chest, and with one broken tusk and a missing ear. Strapped on either side of his chest were skulls and from these hung a number of dried green and red hands.

His reference to the Great Games I had heard so much about while among the Tharks convinced me that I had probably jumped from the frying pan into the fire. After a few more words with the female, during which she assured him that I was now fully fit to travel, the jed ordered that we mount and ride after the main column.

I was strapped securely to a thoat, and with a mounted warrior on either side, we rode off at a furious pace. My wounds gave me little pain, so rapidly had the applications and injections of the female exercised their healing powers, and so deftly had she bound the injuries. Just before dark we reached the main body of troops shortly after they had made camp for the night. I was immediately taken to the leader, who proved to be the jeddak of the hordes of Warhoon.

Like the jed who delivered me to the camp, he was also frightfully scarred and decorated with skulls and dried hands which seemed to mark all the greater warriors among the Warhoons, as well as to indicate their awful ferocity, which is greater even than that of the Tharks.

The jeddak, Bar Comas, who was comparatively young, was the object of the fierce and jealous hatred of his older lieutenant, Dak Kova, the jed who had captured me. I could not miss the almost studied efforts that the latter made to insult his superior.

He entirely omitted the usual formal greeting as we entered the presence of the jeddak, and as he pushed me roughly before the ruler he exclaimed in a loud and menacing voice, "I have brought a strange creature wearing the metal of a Thark and it is my pleasure to have him battle with a wild thoat at the Great Games."

"He will die as Bar Comas, your jeddak, sees fit, if at all!" replied the young ruler, with emphasis and dignity.

"By the dead hands at my throat but he shall die as I say, Bar Comas! No maudlin weakness on your part shall save him. Oh, if only Warhoon were ruled by a real jeddak rather than by a water-hearted weakling from whom even old Dak Kova could tear the metal with his bare hands!"

Bar Comas eyed the defiant and insubordinate chieftain for an instant, his expression one of haughty, fearless contempt and hate, and then without drawing a weapon and without uttering a word he hurled himself at the throat of his defamer.

I had never before seen two green Martian warriors battle with only nature's weapons, and the exhibition of animal ferocity that followed was as fearful a thing as the most disordered imagination could picture. They tore at each others' eyes and ears with their hands and, with their gleaming tusks, repeatedly slashed and gored until both were cut to ribbons from head to foot.

Bar Comas seemed to be winning the battle—he was stronger, quicker and more intelligent. It soon appeared that the encounter was finished except for the final death thrust when Bar Comas slipped and went down. It was the opening that Dak Kova needed, and hurling himself at his adversary he buried his single mighty tusk in Bar Comas's belly and with a last powerful effort ripped the young jeddak wide open the full length of his body, the great tusk finally wedging in the bones of the ex-leader's jaw. Winner and loser both rolled limp and lifeless on the moss, a huge mass of torn and bloody flesh.

Bar Comas was stone dead, and only the most strenuous efforts on the part of Dak Kova's females saved him from the same fate. Three days later he limped to the body of Bar Comas that, by custom, had not been moved from where it fell, and placing his foot upon the neck of his former ruler he assumed the title of Jeddak of Warhoon. The dead jeddak's hands and head were removed and added to the ornaments of his conqueror, and then his women cremated what remained, amid wild and terrible laughter.

My introduction to these cruel and bloodthirsty people was but a preview to the scenes I witnessed almost daily while with them. They are a smaller horde than the Tharks but much more brutal, savage and warlike. Not a day passed without some members of the various Warhoon communities meeting in deadly combat. I have seen as many as eight mortal duels within a single day.

We reached the city of Warhoon after three days on the road and I was immediately cast into a dungeon and securely chained to the floor and walls. Food was brought me at intervals but owing to the utter darkness of the place I do not know whether I lay there days, or weeks, or months. It was the most horrible experience of my life and that my mind did not give way to the terrors of that inky blackness has been a wonder to me ever since. The place was filled with creeping, crawling things; cold, snakelike bodies passed over me when I lay down, and in the darkness I occasionally caught glimpses of gleaming, fiery eyes staring at me. No sound reached me from the world above and no word would my jailer offer when my food was brought to me, although I bombarded him with questions.

Finally all the hatred and loathing I had for these awful creatures that had placed me in this horrible place was centered on this single emissary, my jailer, who, to me, represented the entire horde of Warhoons. I had noticed that he always advanced with his dim torch to where he could place the food within my reach and as he stooped to set it on the floor his head was about level with my chest. So, with the cunning of a madman, I backed into the far corner of my cell when I heard him approaching and, gathering a little slack of the chain in my hand, I waited for him, crouching like some beast of prey. As he bent down to place my food on the ground I swung the chain above my head and crashed the links with all my strength down on his skull. Without a sound he slipped to the floor, dead, and his torch rolled away and went out.

Laughing and chattering like the idiot I was fast becoming, I jumped on his body and felt for his throat. Presently I found the chain at the end of which dangled a number of keys. The touch of my fingers on these keys brought back my reason. No longer was I a babbling maniac, but a sane, reasoning man with the means of escape within my very hands.

As I was groping to remove the chain from around my victim's neck I glanced up into the darkness to see six pairs of gleaming eyes fixed right at me. Slowly they approached and slowly I shrank back from their awful horror. Back into my corner I crouched holding my hands out in front of me, and on came the awful eyes until they reached the dead body at my feet. Then slowly they retreated but this time with a strange grating sound and finally they disappeared into some black and distant recess of my dungeon.

CHAPTER 19

Battling in the Arena

I slowly regained my composure and reached down again to get the keys off the body of my former jailer. But to my horror I found that his body was gone! Then the truth hit me—the owners of those gleaming eyes had dragged my prize away to be devoured in their neighboring lair. They had probably been waiting for days, for weeks, for months—through all this awful eternity of my imprisonment—to drag my dead carcass away to their feast.

For two days I saw no one. No food or water was brought to me as I stayed chained in hunger, darkness, and fear. And then a new jailer appeared and my incarceration went on as before, but I vowed to never again allow my sanity to be crushed by the horror of my imprisonment.

Shortly after this episode another prisoner was brought in and chained near me. By the jailer's dim torchlight I saw that he was a red Martian and I waited impatiently for the guards to leave so I could talk with him. As their retreating footsteps died away in the distance, I called out softly.

"Who are you who speaks out of the darkness?" he answered quietly.

"John Carter, a friend of the red men of Helium."

"I am of Helium," he said, "but I do not recall your name."

And then I told him my story, but leaving out my true feelings for Dejah Thoris. He was excited by the news of Helium's princess and seemed quite positive that she and Sola could have reached safety from where they left me. He said he knew the place well because the Warhoon warriors usually passed through that area when marching to the south.

"Dejah Thoris and Sola entered the hills not five miles from a large waterway and are now probably quite safe," he assured me.

My fellow prisoner was Kantos Kan, a lieutenant in the navy of Helium. He had been a member of the ill-fated expedition that had been attacked by the Tharks at the time of Dejah Thoris's capture, and he briefly related the events that followed the defeat of the battleships.

Badly damaged and only partially manned because of their dead and wounded, the ships had limped back toward Helium. But while passing near the city of Zodanga, the capital of Helium's longtime enemies among the red men of Barsoom, they had been attacked by a large number of war vessels and almost all the surviving Helium craft were either destroyed or captured. His craft was chased for days by the Zodangan warships but finally escaped during the darkness of a moonless night.

Thirty days after the capture of Dejah Thoris, or about the time of our coming to the city of Thark, his vessel had reached Helium with only ten survivors of the original crew. Immediately, several hundred mighty warships along with thousands of smaller support craft were sent out to find Dejah Thoris.

Two green Martian communities had been wiped off the face of Barsoom by the avenging fleets, but no trace of Dejah Thoris had been found. They had been searching among the northern hordes, and only within the past few days had they extended their quest to the south.

Kantos Kan had been assigned to one of the small one-man fliers and was discovered by the Warhoons while exploring their city. The bravery and daring of the man won my respect and admiration. Alone, he had landed at the city's boundary and on foot penetrated to the buildings surrounding the plaza. For two days and nights he had explored their quarters and their dungeons in search of his beloved princess only to fall into the hands of a party of Warhoons as he was about to leave.

Kantos Kan and I became well acquainted and formed a warm personal friendship. Only a few days elapsed, however, before we were dragged from our dungeon for the Great Games. We were led to an amphitheater that held the entire twenty thousand members of the assembled hordes of Warhoon.

The arena was immense and at each end were cages to hold the unfortunate performers until their turns came to meet their horrible death. Kantos Kan and I were confined together in one of the cages. In the others were wild calots, thoats, mad zitidars, green warriors, women of other hordes, and many strange and ferocious wild beasts which I had never seen before. The din of their roaring, growling, and squealing was deafening and the dreadful appearance of any one of the beasts was enough to make the stoutest heart tremble.

Kantos Kan explained to me that during the Great Games, at the end of each day only one of these prisoners would gain freedom and all the others would lie dead in the arena. The winners in the various contests of the day would be pitted against each other until only two remained alive. The victor in the last encounter, whether animal or man, would be set free. The following morning the cages would be filled with a new batch of victims, and so on throughout the ten days of the games.

Shortly after we had been caged, the amphitheater began to fill and within an hour every seat was occupied. Dak Kova, with his jeds and chieftains, sat at the center of one side of the arena on a large raised platform.

At a signal from Dak Kova the doors of two cages were thrown open and a dozen green Martian females were driven out to the center of the arena. Each was given a dagger and then, at the far end, a pack of twelve calots were set loose.

As the brutes, growling and foaming, rushed the almost defenseless women I turned my head. The yells and laughter of the green horde bore witness to the horrible quality of the sport and when I turned back to the arena I saw three victorious calots, snarling and growling over the bodies of their prey. The women had given a good account of themselves. Next, a mad zitidar was set loose among the remaining calots, and so it went throughout the long, hot, horrible day.

During this awful day I was pitted against men and then beasts, but as I was armed with a sword and always outclassed my adversary in agility and strength, the contests were child's play to me. Time and time again I won the applause of the bloodthirsty multitude, and toward the end there were cries that I be taken from the arena and be made a member of the hordes of Warhoon.

Finally there were only three of us left, an immense green warrior of some far northern horde, Kantos Kan, and myself. The other two were to battle first and then I would fight the winner for the freedom that was the award of the final victor.

Kantos Kan had fought several times during the day and like myself had always proven victorious, but occasionally only by the smallest of margins, especially when pitted against the green warriors. I had little hope that he could best his giant adversary who had mowed down everything set against him. The fellow towered over fifteen feet in height, while Kantos Kan was some inches under six feet. As they advanced to meet one another I saw a trick of Martian swordsmanship that gambled Kantos Kan's every hope of victory on one cast of the dice. As he came to within twenty feet of the huge fellow he drew his sword arm far behind him and with a mighty sweep hurled his weapon point first at the green warrior. It flew true as an arrow and, piercing the poor devil's heart, laid him dead on the ground.

Kantos Kan and I were then pitted against each other but as we came together I whispered to him to drag out the battle until nearly dark in the hope that we might find some means of escape. The horde guessed that we did not really want to fight each other and howled in rage as neither of us made a fatal thrust. Just as I saw the sudden coming of dark I whispered to Kantos Kan to thrust his sword between my left arm and my body.

I screamed and staggered back, clasping the sword tightly with my arm, and fell to the ground with his weapon apparently protruding from my chest. Kantos Kan had figured out my trick and, stepping quickly to my side, placed his foot on my neck, drew out his sword and then pretended to give me the final death stroke through the neck. The blow is supposed to sever the jugular vein, but this time the cold blade chopped harmlessly into the sand. In the darkness the crowd thought that he had really finished me. I whispered to him to go and claim his freedom and then look for me in the hills east of the city. After the amphitheater had cleared I crept out quietly, and as the arena lay far from the plaza in an empty portion of the city, I had little trouble in reaching the hills beyond.

CHAPTER 20

In the Atmosphere Factory

For two days I waited in the hills for Kantos Kan, but when he did not show up I started off toward the nearest waterway. My only food consisted of vegetable milk from the plants I occasionally came across. Through two long weeks I wandered, stumbling through the nights guided only by the stars and hiding during the days. Wild beasts attacked me on several occasions. Usually my strange, newly acquired telepathic power warned me in plenty of time, but once in the pitch black dark I was knocked down and had fangs at my jugular before I knew what happened.

I did not know what manner of beast was attacking me, but I could feel that it was large and heavy and many-legged. My hands were at its throat before the fangs had a chance to bury themselves in my neck, and slowly I forced the hairy face away from me and closed my fingers on its windpipe.

Without a sound we lay there, the powerful beast exerting every effort to reach me with those awful fangs, and I straining to maintain my grip and choke out its life as I kept it from my throat. Slowly my arms gave way in the unequal struggle, and inch by inch the burning eyes and gleaming tusks came toward me, until as the hairy face touched mine again, I realized that it was all over. And then, suddenly, a living mass of destruction sprang from the surrounding darkness onto the horrible creature! The two rolled growling on the moss, tearing at one another in a frightful manner, but it was soon over and my rescuer stood with lowered head above the throat of the dead thing that would have killed me.

The nearer moon, rising above the horizon and lighting up the Barsoomian scene, showed me that it was Woola, my faithful hound. Where he had come from, or how he found me, I could not guess. That I was glad, it is needless to say, but my pleasure at seeing him was tempered by anxiety about him leaving Dejah Thoris. I felt that only her death could explain this because he always faithfully followed my commands.

By the light of the now brilliant moons I saw that he was just a shadow of his former self, and as he turned from my caress and commenced greedily to devour the dead carcass at my feet I realized that the poor fellow was more than half starved. I, myself, was in little better plight but I could not bring myself to eat the uncooked flesh and I had no means of making a fire. When Woola had finished his meal I again took up my weary and seemingly endless wandering in quest of the elusive waterway.

At daybreak of the fifteenth day I was overjoyed to see the high trees that usually marked a Barsoomian waterway. As I got closer, I saw an extremely large building hidden by the trees. About noon I dragged myself to the huge structure but the walls showed no opening other than one tiny door. I was about to knock when a voice came from somewhere asking me who I was, where I was from, and the nature of my errand.

I explained that I had escaped from the Warhoons and was dying of starvation and exhaustion.

"You wear the metal of a green warrior and are followed by a calot, yet you look similar to a red man, but in color you are neither green nor red. In the name of the ninth day, what manner of creature are you?"

"I am a friend of the red men of Barsoom and I am starving! Let me enter, I beg you!"

Almost immediately the door slid open, exposing a short, narrow corridor of concrete and another door. No one was in sight, yet as soon as we passed the first door it slid gently back into place behind us. A second and third door slipped to one side, same as the first, before I reached a large inner chamber where I found food and drink set out on a large stone table. The voice directed me to satisfy my hunger and to feed my calot, and while I was thus engaged my invisible host put me through a thorough cross-examination.

"Your statements are most remarkable," said the voice, on concluding the questioning, "but you are evidently speaking the truth, and it is equally evident that you are not of Barsoom. I can tell that by the shape and formation of your brain and the strange location of your internal organs."

"Can you see through me?" I exclaimed.

"Yes, I can see all but your thoughts, and, if you were a Barsoomian, I could read those."

Then a door opened at the far side of the chamber and a strange, dried up little man came in. He wore only a single article of adornment, a small collar of gold from which hung an ornament as large as a dinner plate set solid with huge diamonds, except for the exact center which was occupied by a strange stone, an inch in diameter, that reflected nine different and distinct rays of light. The stone generated the seven colors of our earthly prism and two other beautiful rays that, to me, were new and nameless. I cannot describe them any more than you could describe red to a blind man. I only know that they were beautiful in the extreme.

The old man sat and talked with me for hours, and the strangest part of our discussion was that I could read his every thought while he could not read my mind at all unless I spoke. I did not let him know of my mind reading ability, and thus I learned a great deal which proved very valuable at a later time.

I came to find out that this immense building contained the machinery that produces the artificial atmosphere that sustains life on Mars. The secret of the entire process hinges on the use of the ninth ray, one of the beautiful rays of light that I had noted coming from the center stone in my host's ornament.

This ray is separated from the other rays of the sun by means of finely adjusted instruments placed on the roof of the huge building. The separated ray product is stored in immense tanks that take up almost three fourths of the building's space. This product is then treated electrically, and the result pumped to the five principal air centers of the planet where, as it is released, it transforms into atmosphere. I learned that there is always sufficient reserve of the ninth ray stored in the building to maintain the present Martian atmosphere for a thousand years, and the only fear was that some accident might damage the pumping apparatus.

I was led to an inner chamber where I saw a group of twenty radium pumps that furnish Mars with the atmosphere compound. He told me he had been monitoring these pumps for eight hundred years. He has one assistant who shares the task with him and for half a Martian year, each of these men is alone in this huge, isolated plant.

Every red Martian is taught the principles of the manufacture of atmosphere, but only two at one time ever hold the secret of entering the building, which is built with walls a hundred and fifty feet thick and is absolutely unassailable. All Barsoomians realize that the existence of every form of life of Mars is dependent on the uninterrupted working of this plant.

One curious fact I discovered as I watched his thoughts was that the outer doors are opened and closed by telepathic means. The locks are so finely adjusted that the doors are released by the action of a certain combination of thought waves. I asked him in a casual manner how he had managed to unlock the massive doors for me from the inner chambers of the building. As quick as a flash there came to his mind the nine Martian sounds for the entry key, but these quickly faded as he answered that this was a secret he must not divulge.

From then on his manner toward me changed as though he feared that he had been tricked into divulging a great secret, and I read suspicion and fear in his looks and thoughts, though his words were still pleasant. Before I retired for the night he promised to give me a letter to a nearby agricultural officer who would help me on my way to Zodanga, which was the nearest Martian city.

"But do not let them know your destination is Helium because they are at war with that country. My assistant and I are of no country, we belong to all Barsoom and this talisman which we wear protects us in all lands, even among the green men—though we do not trust them. And so goodnight, my friend," he continued, "may you have a long and restful sleep—yes, a long sleep."

And, though he smiled pleasantly, I saw in his thoughts the wish that he had never admitted me into his building. Next I saw a mental picture of him standing over me in the night and the swift thrust of a dagger and the half formed words, "I am sorry, but it is for the good of Barsoom." He then left the room and any further reading of his thoughts stopped.

What was I to do? How could I escape through these thick walls? I could kill him easily now that I was warned, but once he was dead, could I make my escape? And with him dead, the machinery of the great plant might stop and I would die along with all the other inhabitants of the planet. For the others I did not give the snap of my finger, but the thought of harm to Dejah Thoris drove from my mind all desire to kill my mistaken host.

Cautiously I opened the door of my apartment, and followed by Woola, looked for the doors to the outside. A wild scheme had come to me; I would attempt to force the locks by the nine thought waves I had read in my host's mind.

Creeping quietly through corridor after corridor and down winding runways I finally reached the great hall where I had broken my long fast that morning. Nowhere had I seen my host, nor did I know where he kept himself at night. I was just about to step out into the room when a noise warned me and I slipped back into the shadows dragging Woola after me.

Soon the old man passed by, and as he entered the dim chamber I saw that he held a long thin dagger and was sharpening it on a stone. In his mind was the thought to inspect the radium pumps, which would take about thirty minutes, and then return to my bed chamber and finish me off. After he passed on his way, I left my hiding place and crossed to the door—the inner of the three that stood between me and the outside.

Concentrating my mind on the lock I hurled the nine thought waves against it. I waited, and finally the door moved softly and slid quietly to one side. One after the other the remaining portals opened at my command and Woola and I stepped out into the darkness, free, but little better off than we had been before, aside from our full stomachs.

I made for the first crossroad, intending to get to the central turnpike as quickly as possible. This I reached about morning and after a few miles I spotted a few structures on the side of the road. These were low rambling buildings of concrete barred with heavy doors, and no amount of hammering brought any response. Weary and exhausted from sleeplessness I threw myself on the ground and ordered Woola to stand guard.

Some time later I was awakened by his growling and opened my eyes to see three red Martians covering me with their rifles. "I am unarmed and no enemy," I quickly explained. "I have been a prisoner among the green men and am on my way to Zodanga. All I ask is food and rest and directions to my destination."

They lowered their rifles and advanced pleasantly toward me and placed their right hands on my left shoulder. I had previously learned from Kantos Kan, that this is how they greet one another. They then took me to a house only a short distance away.

The buildings I had seen that morning were for stock animals and farm machinery. This residence dwelling was standing among a grove of enormous trees. Like most red-Martian homes, it had been raised at night some fifty feet from the ground on a large round metal shaft. This shaft slid up or down inside a sleeve sunk in the ground, and was operated by a tiny radium engine in the entrance hall of the building. Instead of bothering with strong doors, bolts, and bars to secure their dwellings, the red Martians simply raise them up out of harm's way during the night.

These men, all brothers, along with their wives and children, occupied three similar houses on this farm. They did no farm work themselves, being government officers in charge. The actual labor was performed by convicts and prisoners of war. The officers were perfect examples of hospitality and I spent several days with them, resting and recuperating from my experiences.

When they had heard my story—I omitted all reference to Dejah Thoris and the old man of the atmosphere plant—they advised me to color my body to more nearly resemble their own race and then attempt to find employment in Zodanga.

"The chances are small that your tale will be believed until after you have proven your trustworthiness and won friends among the higher nobles of the court. This you can most easily do through military service, as we are a warlike people," explained one of them.

When I was ready to depart they furnished me with a small domestic bull thoat, used for saddle purposes by all red Martians. The animal was the size of a horse and quite gentle, but in color and shape was an exact replica of his huge and fierce wild cousin.

The brothers had supplied me with a red colored oil which I used to stain my entire body. After this they said I could pass anywhere on Barsoom as a full-fledged red Martian. I was outfitted in the style of a Zodangan gentleman and given a letter of introduction. Bidding me farewell, they watched me until I was out of sight on the broad turnpike.

CHAPTER 21

An Air Scout for Zodanga

As I proceeded on my journey toward Zodanga many strange and interesting sights came to my attention, and at the several farm houses where I stopped I learned a number of new and instructive things concerning Barsoom.

The water that supplies the farms and cities of Mars is collected in immense underground reservoirs and pumped through long pipelines to the various population centers. Along the entire length of these conduits lie the cultivated districts. These are divided into tracts of about the same size, each tract being under the supervision of government officers.

Instead of flooding the surface of the fields, and thus wasting immense quantities of water by evaporation, the precious liquid is carried underground through a vast network of small pipes directly to the roots of the vegetation. The crops on Mars are always uniform, for there are no droughts, no rains, and no high winds.

On this trip I tasted the first meat I had eaten since leaving Earth—large, juicy steaks and chops from the well-fed domestic animals of the farms. Also I enjoyed luscious fruits and vegetables.

At another stop I met some highly refined people of the noble class and during our conversation the topic of Helium was mentioned. One of the older men had been there on a diplomatic mission and spoke about the conditions that seemed to always keep these two cities at war.

Changing the subject, he said, "Helium boasts the most beautiful women of Barsoom, and of all her treasures the princess, Dejah Thoris, is the most exquisite flower." He added, "the people worship the ground she walks on and since her loss on that ill-fated expedition all Helium has been draped in mourning.

"That our ruler should have attacked the disabled fleet as it was returning to Helium was another of his blunders which will sooner or later compel Zodanga to elevate a wiser man to his place. Even now, though our victorious armies are surrounding Helium, the people of Zodanga are voicing their displeasure, for the war is not a popular one, since it is not based on right or justice. Our forces took advantage when their fleet was searching for the princess, and so we have been able to reduce the city to a sorry plight. It is said it will fall within the next few passages of the further moon."

"And what do you think may have happened to the princess, Dejah Thoris?" I asked as casually as possible.

"No one knows," he answered sadly. "Some say she was killed in the southern desert, some say she escaped from the hordes of Thark with a strange creature of another world, only to fall into the hands of the Warhoons."

While this information was in no way reassuring, it did not prove the death of Dejah Thoris. I decided to make every effort to reach Helium as quickly as I could and report to Tardos Mors my news of his granddaughter's possible whereabouts.

Ten days after leaving the three Ptor brothers I arrived at Zodanga. Since the red men of Mars never domesticated the calot I knew that Woola would draw unwelcome attention. The thought of parting with my faithful companion caused me such sorrow that I put it off until just before we arrived at the city's gates; but then, finally, it became imperative that we separate. If it had been only for my own safety, no argument could have caused me to send away the one creature on Barsoom that had never failed me in affection and loyalty.

But I would willingly offer my life for Dejah

Thoris and I was about to challenge the unknown dangers of this mysterious city, so it was time for us to separate. And so I told the poor beast farewell, promising him that I would search for him if I came through this safely. It was hard to watch him go but I set off toward Zodanga and with a touch of heartsickness, approached her towering walls.

The letter from the Ptor brothers gained me entrance to the vast, walled city. It was still very early in the morning and the streets were practically deserted. The residences, raised high up on their metal columns, resembled huge birdhouses, while the uprights themselves presented the appearance of steel tree trunks. The shops as a rule were not raised from the ground, since thievery is practically unknown on Barsoom.

The brothers had given me directions to find both living accommodations and the government offices that might assist me. My way led to the central square or plaza, which is a characteristic of all Martian cities. The plaza of Zodanga covers a square mile and is surrounded by the palaces of the jeddak, the jeds, and other members of the royalty of Zodanga, as well as by the principal public buildings, cafes, and shops.

As I was crossing the immense square, lost in wonder and admiration at the magnificent architecture and the gorgeous vegetation carpeting the broad lawns, I spotted a red Martian walking briskly toward me from one of the avenues. He did not notice me, but as he came closer I recognized him, and reached my hand out to his shoulder saying, "Kantos Kan!"

Like lightning he wheeled and before I could so much as lower my hand the point of his sword was leveled at my chest. "Who are you?" he growled, and then as a backward leap carried me fifty feet from his sword he dropped the point to the ground and laughed, "I do not need a better reply, there is only one man on all Barsoom who can bounce about like a rubber ball. By the mother of the further moon, John Carter, how did you get here, and are you now able to change your color at will?

"You gave me a bad moment my friend," he continued quietly, after I had briefly outlined my adventures since parting with him in the arena at Warhoon. "If my name and city were known to the Zodangans I would quickly be sitting on the banks of the lost sea of Korus with my revered and departed ancestors and my severed head in my lap. I am here in the interest of Tardos Mors, Jeddak of Helium, to discover the whereabouts of Dejah Thoris, our princess. Sab Than, prince of Zodanga, has her hidden in the city and has fallen madly in love with her.

"His father, Than Kosis, Jeddak of Zodanga, has insisted that she marry his son as the price of peace between our cities, but Tardos Mors will not accede to the demand. Her father has sent word that he and his people would rather see their princess dead than have her wed to any man other than one of her own choice. His reply was the deadliest affront he could have put to Than Kosis and the Zodangans, but his people love him for it and his strength in Helium is greater today than ever.

"I have been here three days," continued Kantos Kan, "but I have not yet found where Dejah Thoris is imprisoned. Today I join the Zodangan navy as an air scout and I hope to win the confidence of Sab Than, the prince, who is commander of this division of the navy, and thus learn the whereabouts of Dejah Thoris. I am glad that you are here, John Carter, for I know you are loyal to my princess and the two of us working together should be able to accomplish a great deal."

Kantos Kan took me to the headquarters of the air scout squadron and asked that I be enrolled as a member of the corps. The next few days were spent teaching me the methods of flying and repairing the dainty little flying machines. The body of the one-man aircraft is about sixteen feet long and two feet wide, tapering to a point at each end. The driver sits on a seat constructed over the small, noiseless radium engine. Buoyancy tanks are contained inside the thin metal walls of the ship and contain the eighth

Barsoomian ray, or ray of propulsion, as it is called.

This ray, like the ninth ray, is unknown on Earth, but the Martians have discovered that it is an inherent property of all light. They have learned that this solar eighth ray propels the light of the sun to the various planets, and that it is the planet's eighth ray that "reflects," or propels the light back out into space. The solar eighth ray would be absorbed by the surface of Barsoom, but the Barsoomian eighth ray is constantly streaming out from the planet. This ray makes a force of anti-gravity which, when controlled, is able to lift enormous weights. This has enabled them to perfect aviation and allow battleships to sail as gracefully and lightly through the thin air of Barsoom as a toy balloon.

The fourth day after my arrival at Zodanga I made my first, and as it turned out, most important flight. I rose above the city, circled it several times, and then, throwing my engine into top speed, I raced to the south, following one of the great waterways.

I had traveled two hundred miles in a little less than an hour when I looked down and saw three green warriors racing madly on their thoats toward a small figure who seemed to be trying to escape. Dropping my machine rapidly toward them, and circling behind the warriors, I soon saw that the object of their pursuit was a red

Martian wearing the metal of my new air scout squadron. His damaged flying machine was a short distance away.

They were now almost on him; their swift mounts charging down on the relatively puny figure at terrific speed, while the warriors leaned low with their long metal-shod spears reaching out toward my comrade-in-arms. Each was trying to be the first to impale the poor Zodangan and in another moment his fate would have been sealed.

Driving my aircraft toward the warriors I soon overtook them and rammed the prow of my little flier between the shoulders of the closest one. The impact hurled the fellow's head to one side and his decapitated body sprawled in the moss. The mounts of the other two warriors squealed in terror and ran off in opposite directions.

Reducing my speed I circled and landed at the feet of the astonished Zodangan. We wasted no time in talk, knowing that the warriors would return. After quickly flying back to his damaged machine we were trying to finish the repairs when we saw the two green monsters attacking at top speed. When they got close, their thoats again became unmanageable and refused to advance toward the frightening aircraft. The warriors finally dismounted and advanced toward us on foot with drawn swords.

I ran to meet the larger warrior, telling the

Zodangan to do the best he could with the other one. Finishing my man with almost no effort, I quickly returned to my new acquaintance and found him in desperate straits. He was wounded and down on his back with the enemy's sword raised to deal the final thrust. With a bound, I cleared the fifty feet between us and drove my sword completely through the body of the green warrior.

A cursory examination revealed no mortal injuries to the Zodangan and after a brief rest he said he felt fit enough for the return voyage. He would have to pilot his own craft, however, as these frail vessels are not intended to carry more than a single person for any length of time. Quickly completing the repairs we flew together into the still, cloudless Martian sky and returned to Zodanga.

As we neared the city, we discovered an immense gathering of civilians and troops. The sky was black with naval vessels and private aircraft, flying long streamers of brightly colored silks, banners, and flags.

My companion signaled and suggested that we watch the ceremony. He then unfurled the ensign of the royal family of Zodanga and we made our way through the maze of low flying air vessels until we hovered directly over the Jeddak of Zodanga and his staff. All were mounted on the small domestic bull thoats of the red

Martians, and their trappings and ornamentation displayed so many gorgeously colored feathers that I was struck by the startling resemblance the scene bore to a band of the wild west Indians of my own Earth.

One of the staff pointed out my companion to Than Kosis and the ruler motioned for him to descend. As they waited for the troops to move into position facing the jeddak, the two talked earnestly together, the jeddak and his staff occasionally glancing up at me. Presently they all dismounted and observed the spectacle of the marching soldiers until the last body of troops had moved into position in front of their emperor. A member of the staff advanced toward the troops, and calling out the name of a soldier, commanded him to advance. The officer then recited the nature of the heroic act that had won the approval of the jeddak, who then placed a metal ornament on the left arm of the lucky man.

Ten men had been awarded their decorations when the officer called out, "John Carter, air scout!"

Never in my life had I been so surprised, but my military discipline is strong, and I dropped my little machine lightly to the ground and advanced on foot as I had seen the others do. As I halted in front of the officer, he addressed me in a voice audible to the entire assembly of troops and spectators.

"In recognition of your remarkable courage and skill in defending the person of the cousin of the Jeddak, Than Kosis, and vanquishing three green warriors, it is his pleasure to confer on you the mark of his gratitude!"

Than Kosis then advanced, and placing an ornament on me, said: "My cousin has reported the details of your wonderful achievement. If you can defend a cousin of the jeddak so well, I am sure you could do even better defending the jeddak himself. You are therefore appointed a lieutenant of The Guards and will be quartered in my palace."

I thanked him, and at his direction joined the members of his staff. After the ceremony I returned my machine to its quarters on the roof at the air scout squadron, and with an orderly to guide me, we marched to the palace and I reported to the officer in charge.

CHAPTER 22

I Find Dejah Thoris

The officer assigned me to a station near the jeddak, who in time of war, is always in great danger of assassination. The rule that "all is fair in war" seems to constitute the entire ethics of Martian conflict. He escorted me to an apartment where the jeddak was engaged in conversation with his son, Sab Than, and several attendants. No one noticed our entrance.

The walls of the large apartment appeared to be covered with splendid tapestries hiding all the windows and doors. My guide drew aside one of the tapestries, revealing a pathway that encircled the room between the hangings and the actual walls of the chamber. He told me to patrol this area as long as Than Kosis was inside the apartment. When the jeddak left, I was to follow him discreetly. My only duty was to guard the ruler and keep out of sight as much as possible.

The tapestries were of a strange cloth that gave the appearance of heavy fabric from one side, but from my assigned area I could look right through them and easily observe all that took place inside the room. I was only at my post a short time when the tapestry at the opposite end of the chamber separated and four soldiers surrounding a female figure entered the apartment. As they approached Than Kosis, the soldiers spread out to reveal Dejah Thoris, standing in front of the jeddak!

Sab Than, Prince of Zodanga, advanced to meet her, and taking her hand with affection, they approached the jeddak. Than Kosis looked up in surprise, rose to his feet, saluted her and said, "To what do I owe this visit from the Princess of Helium, who previously assured me that she would prefer Tal Hajus, the green Thark, to my son?"

Dejah Thoris smiled and answered, "From the beginning of time upon Barsoom it has been the privilege of a woman to change her mind and to hide her true thoughts in matters concerning her heart. That you will forgive, Than Kosis, as has your son. Two days ago I was not sure of his love for me, but now I am, and I have come to beg you to forget my rash words and to accept the assurance of the Princess of Helium that when the time comes she will wed Sab Than, Prince of Zodanga."

"I am glad that you have so decided," replied Than Kosis. "It is far from my desire to push war further against the people of Helium, and your promise shall be recorded and a proclamation to my people issued immediately."

"It would be better, Than Kosis," interrupted Dejah Thoris, "that the proclamation wait until the ending of this war. It would look strange to my people and to yours if the Princess of Helium were to give herself to her country's enemy in the midst of hostilities."

"Cannot the war be ended at once?" asked Sab Than. "It requires but the word of Than Kosis to bring peace. Say it, my father, say the word that will hasten my happiness, and end this unpopular conflict."

"We shall see how the people of Helium react to a proposal for peace. I shall offer it to them immediately," was the reply.

Dejah Thoris, after a few words, turned and left the apartment, still followed by her guards.

And so my brief dream of happiness was dashed to the ground of reality. The woman for whom I had offered my life, and from whose lips I had so recently heard a declaration of love, had forgotten my very existence and given herself to the son of her people's most hated enemy.

Although I had heard it with my own ears, I could not believe it. I must hear her repeat the cruel truth to me alone before I would be convinced, and so I deserted my post and dashed through the passage behind the tapestries toward the door where she had left the chamber. Slipping quietly through this opening, I discovered a maze of winding corridors, branching and turning in every direction.

Running rapidly down first one and then another, I soon became hopelessly lost and was standing panting next to a wall when I heard voices near me. Apparently they were coming from the opposite side of the partition and I soon made out the voice of Dejah Thoris. I could not hear the words but I knew the voice. Moving a few steps, I discovered another passageway ending at a door. Walking boldly forward I pushed into the room only to find myself in a small chamber occupied by the four guards I had just seen. One of them arose and asked the nature of my business.

"I am from Than Kosis," I replied, "and wish to speak privately with Dejah Thoris, Princess of Helium."

"And your orders?" asked the fellow.

I did not know what he meant, but replied that I was a member of The Guard, and without waiting I strode toward the opposite door of the chamber, behind which I could hear Dejah Thoris. But the guardsman stepped in front of me, saying, "No one comes from Than Kosis without carrying orders or the password. You must give me one or the other before you may pass."

"My friend, the only order I require to enter where I will, hangs at my side," I answered, tapping my sword. "Will you let me pass in peace or not?"

For reply he whipped out his own sword, calling to the others to join him, and thus the four stood, with drawn weapons, barring my further progress. "You are not here by the order of Than Kosis," cried the one who had first addressed me, "and not only shall you not enter the apartments of the Princess of Helium but you shall go back to Than Kosis under guard to explain yourself. Throw down your sword! You cannot hope to overcome four of us," he added with a grim smile.

My reply was a quick thrust that left me with only three antagonists and I can assure you that they were worthy of my metal. They had me backed against the wall in no time, fighting for my life. Slowly I worked my way to a corner of the room where I could force them to come at me only one at a time, and thus we fought for almost twenty minutes; the clanging of steel on steel producing a veritable bedlam in the little room.

The noise brought Dejah Thoris to the door of her apartment, and there she stood throughout the conflict with Sola peering over her. Her face was set and emotionless and I knew that she did not recognize me, nor did Sola. Finally a lucky cut brought down a second guardsman and then, with only two opposing me, I changed my tactics and rushed them. The third fell within ten seconds after the second, and the last lay dead on the bloody floor a few moments later.

They were brave men and noble fighters, and it grieved me that I had been forced to kill them, but I would have willingly depopulated all Barsoom to reach the side of my Dejah Thoris. Sheathing my bloody blade I advanced toward my Martian Princess, who still stood mutely gazing at me without sign of recognition.

"Who are you, Zodangan?" she whispered. "Another enemy to harass me in my misery?"

"I am a friend, a once cherished friend."

"No friend of Helium's princess wears that metal . . . and yet the voice! I have heard it before; it is no—it cannot be—no, for he is dead!"

"It is ME, my Princess, none other than John Carter," I said. "Do you not recognize, even through paint and strange metal, the heart of your chieftain?"

As I came close to her she swayed toward me with outstretched hands, but as I reached to take her in my arms she drew back with a shudder and a little moan of misery. "Too late, too late," she grieved. "O my chieftain that was, and whom I thought dead, had you but returned one little hour before—but now it is too late, too late."

"What do you mean? Do you mean that you would not have promised yourself to the Zodangan prince had you known that I lived?"

"Oh, John Carter, do you think that I would give my heart to you yesterday and today give it to another? I thought that it lay buried with your ashes in the pits of Warhoon, and so today I have promised my body to another to save my people from the curse of a victorious Zodangan army."

"But I am not dead, my princess. I have come to claim you, and all Zodanga cannot prevent it!"

"It is too late, John Carter, my promise is given, and on Barsoom that is final. The ceremonies that follow later are but meaningless formalities. They make the fact of marriage no more certain than does the funeral cortege of a jeddak again place the seal of death upon him. I am as good as married, John Carter. No longer may you call me your princess. No longer are you my chieftain."

"I know but little of your customs here upon Barsoom, Dejah Thoris, but I do know that I love you, and if you meant the last words you spoke to me that day as the hordes of Warhoon were charging down upon us, no other man shall ever claim you as his bride. You meant them then, my princess, and you mean them still. Say that it is true."

"I meant them, John Carter," she whispered. "I cannot repeat them now for I have given myself to another. Ah, if you had only known our ways, my friend," she continued, half to herself, "the promise would have been yours long months ago, and you could have claimed me before all others. It might have meant the fall of Helium, but I would have given my empire for you, my Tharkian chief."

Then aloud she said: "Do you remember the night when you offended me? You called me your princess without having asked for my hand, and then you boasted that you had fought for me. You did not know this was improper, and I should not have been offended—I see that now. But there was no one to tell you that upon Barsoom there are two kinds of women in the cities of the red men. The one they fight for that they may ask for them in marriage; the other kind they fight for also, but without such noble purpose. When a man has won a woman he may address her as his princess, or in any of the other terms that signify possession.

"You had fought for me, but had never asked for me in marriage, and so when you called me your princess, you see . . ." she faltered, "I was hurt, but even then, John Carter, I did not repulse you, as I should have done, until you made it doubly worse by taunting me with having won me through combat."

"I do not need ask your forgiveness now, Dejah Thoris. You must know that my fault was in ignorance of your Barsoomian customs. What I failed to do, because I thought my petition would be unwelcome, I do now. Dejah Thoris, I ask you to be my wife, and by all the Virginian fighting blood that flows in my veins you shall be."

"No, John Carter, it is useless," she cried, hopelessly, "I may never be yours while Sab Than lives."

"You have sealed his death warrant, my princess—Sab Than dies."

"No! That must not happen either," she hastened to explain. "I may not wed the man who slays my husband, even in self-defense. It is custom. We are ruled by custom upon Barsoom. It is useless, my friend. You must bear the sorrow with me. That, at least, we may share in common. That, and the memory of our brief days among the Tharks. You must go now, and must never see me again. Goodbye, my chieftain that was."

Disheartened and dejected, I withdrew from the room, but I was not entirely discouraged, nor would I admit that Dejah Thoris was lost to me until the ceremony had actually been performed. As I wandered along the corridors, I knew that my only hope lay in escape from the city of Zodanga, for the matter of the four dead guardsmen would have to be explained.

After a while I came to the doorway of a large apartment containing a number of guardsmen. The walls of this room were also hung with transparent tapestries and I was able to hide myself. The guardsmen talked quietly until an officer entered and ordered four of the men to relieve the detail who were guarding the Princess of Helium. Now, I knew my troubles would start in earnest. It seemed that the squad had just left the guardroom when one of them burst back in again shouting that they had found their four comrades butchered at their post.

In a moment the entire palace was alive with people. Guardsmen, officers, servants, and slaves ran helter-skelter through the corridors and apartments carrying messages and orders, and searching for signs of the intruders. This was my opportunity, and slim as it was, I grabbed it. As a number of soldiers came hurrying past my hiding place I trailed behind and followed them through the mazes of the palace until I saw a series of large windows.

Here I left my guides, and slipping to the nearest window, sought an avenue of escape. The window overlooked one of the broad avenues of Zodanga. The ground was about thirty feet below and a short distance from the building was a wall twenty feet high. To a red Martian, escape by this path would have appeared impossible, but to me, with my earthly strength and agility, it would be child's play. My only fear was getting caught before darkness—I knew I could not make the leap in broad daylight while the court below and the avenue beyond were crowded with Zodangans.

So I found a hiding place inside a huge hanging ornament suspended from the ceiling. I jumped up to the bowl-like vase and had just settled down inside when I heard a number of people enter the room. The group stopped beneath me and I could plainly overhear their every word.

"It is the work of Heliumites," said someone with an air of authority.

"Yes, O Jeddak, but how did they get into the palace? I believe that a single enemy might reach the inner chambers, but how a force of six or eight fighting men could have done so with no one seeing them is beyond me. We shall soon know, however, for here comes the royal psychologist."

Another man now joined the group, and after making his formal greetings to his ruler, said: "O mighty Jeddak, it is a strange tale I read in the minds of your faithful dead guardsmen. They were felled not by a number of fighting men, but by a single opponent."

He paused to let the full weight of this announcement sink in. His unbelievable statement was greeted with skepticism as Than Kosis snarled, "What manner of weird tale are you bringing me?"

"It is the truth, my Jeddak," replied the psychologist. "In fact the impressions were strongly marked on the brain of each of the four guardsmen. Their antagonist was a very tall man, wearing the metal of one of your own guardsmen, and his fighting ability was little short of marvelous for he fought fair against the entire four and overcame them all by his skill and superhuman strength and endurance. Though he wore the metal of Zodanga, my Jeddak, such a man was never seen before in this or any other country on Barsoom.

"I also questioned the Princess of Helium. Her mind was blank to me; she has perfect control of her thoughts and I could not read anything. She did say that she witnessed a portion of the encounter, and saw only one man engaged with the guardsmen."

"Where is John Carter who saved me from the green monsters?" spoke another of the party, and I recognized the voice of the ruler's cousin from this afternoon's adventure. "By the metal of my first ancestor, the description fits him to perfection, especially as to his fighting ability."

"Where is this man?" cried Than Kosis. "Have him brought to me at once. What do you know about him, cousin? It seems strange that there would be such a fighting man in Zodanga and we didn't know about him before today."

It was soon reported that I was nowhere to

be found, either in the palace or at the air scout squadron. They found Kantos Kan and questioned him, but he knew nothing of my whereabouts, and as to my past, he had told them he knew nothing, since he had but recently met me during our captivity among the Warhoons.

"Keep your eyes on this other one," commanded Than Kosis. "He is a stranger also and likely as not they both hail from Helium, and where one is we shall sooner or later find the other. Quadruple the air patrol, and have every man who leaves the city be subjected to the closest scrutiny."

Another messenger now entered with word that I was still inside the palace. "The likeness of every person who has left the palace grounds today has been carefully examined," concluded the fellow, "and not one looked like this new lieutenant of the guards."

"Then we will have him shortly," commented Than Kosis contentedly, "and in the meanwhile we will go to the apartments of the Princess of Helium and question her again. She may know more than she cared to tell us at first. Come."

They left the hall, and as darkness fell, I slipped from my hiding place and went to the balcony. Few men were in sight, and choosing a moment when no one seemed near, I sprang quickly to the top of the wall and from there to the avenue beyond the palace grounds.

CHAPTER 23

Lost in the Sky

I ran toward our quarters, where I felt sure I would find Kantos Kan. As I neared the building I became more careful, thinking that the place would be heavily guarded. Several men in civilian metal loitered near the front and rear entrances. My only means of reaching the upper story to our apartments was through an adjoining building, and after considerable maneuvering I managed to get to the roof of a shop several doors away.

Leaping from roof to roof, I soon reached an open window in the building where I hoped to find my friend from Helium, and in another moment I stood in the room with him. Halfway through my account of the events he was very excited, but then the news that Dejah Thoris had promised her hand to Sab Than filled him with dismay.

"It cannot be! It is impossible! Any man in Helium would prefer death to the selling of our beloved princess to the ruling house of Zodanga. She must have lost her mind to go along with such a bargain. You, who do not know how we love our ruling family in Helium, cannot imagine what we would think of such an unholy alliance! What can be done, John Carter? You are a resourceful man. Can you think of some way to save our princess from this disgrace?"

"If I can come within sword's reach of Sab Than," I answered, "I can solve the difficulty, but for personal reasons I would prefer that another struck the blow that frees Dejah Thoris."

Kantos Kan eyed me narrowly before he spoke, "You love her! Does she know it?"

"She knows it, my friend, and rejects me only because she has promised herself to Sab Than."

The splendid fellow sprang to his feet, and grasping me by the shoulder with one hand, raised his sword with the other and exclaimed, "And had the choice been left to me I could not have chosen a more fitting mate for the first princess of Barsoom. Here is my hand upon your shoulder, John Carter, and my word that Sab Than shall go out at the point of my sword for the sake of my love for Helium, for Dejah Thoris, and for you. This very night I shall try to reach his quarters in the palace!"

"How?" I asked. "You are strongly guarded

and a quadruple force patrols the sky."

For a moment he bent his head in thought, and then raised it with an air of confidence. "I only need to pass these guards and I can do it. I know a secret entrance to the palace through the highest tower. I stumbled on it by chance one day as I was passing above the palace on patrol duty. If I can reach the roof of the aircraft head-quarters and get my machine, I can be in Sab Than's apartment in five minutes; but how am I to escape from this building?"

"How well are the aircraft hangers guarded?" I asked.

"There is usually only one man on duty at night."

"Go up to the roof of this building, Kantos Kan, and wait for me there."

Without stopping to explain my plans I retraced my way to the street and hurried back to headquarters. It was so well guarded I did not dare enter the building from any of its ground floor entrances. The building was enormous, rearing its lofty head fully a thousand feet into the air. I knew it would be a long, dangerous climb up the face of the building, but there was no other way. The fact that the architecture of Zodanga is extremely ornate made the feat sim-pler than I had anticipated, since I found orna-mental ledges and projections that allowed me to easily get all the way up to the eaves at the top of the building. But here I met my first real obstacle—the eaves projected nearly twenty feet out from the wall.

The top floor was all lit up and filled with fighting men; I knew I could not reach the roof that way. There was one slight, desperate chance, and I decided I must take it—it was for Dejah Thoris, and I would risk a thousand deaths for her.

Clinging to the wall with one hand, I unfastened one of the straps and hooks of my uniform's trappings. I swung the hook cautiously up to the roof several times before it finally found a grip. Then I gently pulled on it to strengthen its hold, but I did not know if it would bear my weight. For just an instant I hesitated, and then, releasing my grip on the wall, I swung out into space at the end of the strap! Far below me lay the brilliantly lit streets, the hard pavement, and death. There was a little jerk at the top of the supporting overhang, and a nasty slipping, grating sound that turned me cold with apprehension; then the hook caught again and I was safe.

Clambering quickly aloft I grasped the edge of the roof and drew myself up to the surface above. As I gained my feet, I was confronted by the sentry on duty and stared into the muzzle of his pistol.

"Who are you and where did you come from?" he demanded.

"I am an air scout, friend, and very near a dead one, for just by the merest chance I escaped falling to the avenue below!"

"But how did you get up on the roof, man? No one has landed or come up from the building for the past hour. Quick, explain yourself, or I call the guard!"

"Look here, sentry, and you shall see how I got up and how close I came to not getting here at all," I answered, turning toward the edge, where twenty feet below, at the end of my strap, hung all my weapons.

The fellow, acting on impulse, stepped to my side and to his undoing, for as he leaned to peer over the eaves I grabbed him by his throat and his pistol arm and threw him to the roof's surface. The weapon dropped from his grasp and my fingers choked off his attempted cry for help. I gagged and bound him and then hung him over the edge of the roof as I myself had hung a few moments before. I knew it would be morning before he would be discovered, and I needed all the time that I could get.

Donning my trappings and weapons I ran to the sheds, and soon had prepared both my machine and Kantos Kan's. Attaching his aircraft behind mine I started my engine, and skimming over the edge of the roof I dove down into the streets of the city, far below the level usually occupied by the air patrol. In less than a minute

I was settling safely on the roof of our building beside the astonished Kantos Kan.

We quickly formed our plan. I was to try to lure the patrols away and race toward Helium while Kantos Kan was to enter the palace and dispatch Sab Than. If successful, he was then to follow me and we would regroup, get help, and come back for the princess. After a quick good-luck salute we rose together and sped off in the direction of the palace.

As we neared the high tower, a patrol flew down from above throwing its piercing search-light on my craft, and a voice roared out a command to halt, followed with a shot. Kantos Kan dropped quickly into the darkness while I pointed my craft's nose to the sky and raced through the Martian night followed by a dozen of the air scout craft. By twisting and turning my little machine, rising and now falling, I managed to elude their search-lights most of the time, but I was also losing ground by these tactics, and so I decided to hazard everything on a straight-away course and leave the result to fate and the speed of my machine.

Kantos Kan had shown me a trick of gearing, which is known only to the navy of Helium, that greatly increased the speed of our machines so that I felt sure I could outrun my pursuers if I could dodge their projectiles for just a few more moments.

As I sped through the air, the screeching of the bullets around me convinced me that only by a miracle could I escape, but the die was cast, and throwing the lever to full speed I raced in a straight course toward Helium. Gradually I left my pursuers further and further behind and I was congratulating myself on my lucky escape when a well-directed—or extremely lucky—shot exploded at the front of my little craft. The concussion nearly capsized her, and with a sickening jerk she plunged downward through the dark night.

How far I fell before I regained control of the machine I do not know, but I must have been very close to the ground. As I started to rise again I heard the squealing of animals below me in the dark. Gaining altitude, I scanned the heavens for my pursuers, finally making out their lights far behind me where they were landing to search for me.

When I judged them far enough away, I flashed my lamp on my compass and found that a fragment of the projectile had destroyed my only guide, as well as my speedometer. It was true I could follow the stars in the general direction of Helium, but without knowing the exact direction to the city, or the speed at which I was traveling, my chances for finding it were slim.

Helium lies a thousand miles southwest of Zodanga, and with my compass intact I could have made the trip, barring accidents, in between four and five hours. As it turned out, however, morning found me speeding over a vast expanse of dead sea bottom after nearly six hours of continuous flight at high speed. Suddenly I saw a very large city below me, but it was not my goal, as Helium, alone of all the cities on Barsoom, consists of two immense circular walled cities a short distance apart, each with an incredibly high tower. The two towers, one of vivid scarlet rising nearly a mile into the air and her sister, a bright yellow and of the same height, would have been easily distinguishable from my altitude.

Believing that I had come too far to the north and west, I turned back in a southeasterly direction, passing several other large cities, but none resembling Helium.

Tars Tarkas Finds a Friend

About noon I passed low over an ancient dead city and came upon several thousand green warriors engaged in a terrific battle. Scarcely had I seen them than a volley of shots was directed at me, and with their unfailing accuracy, my little craft was instantly a ruined wreck, sinking erratically to the ground.

I fell almost directly into the center of the fierce combat among fighting warriors who had not seen my approach. The men were fighting on foot with swords, while an occasional shot from a sharpshooter on the outskirts of the conflict would bring down a warrior who found himself separated from the entangled mass.

As my machine sank among them, I realized that it was fight or die—with good chances of dying in any event—and so I struck the ground with drawn sword ready to defend myself as best I could.

I fell beside a huge monster who was engaged with three of his enemies, and as I glanced at his fierce face filled with the light of battle, I recognized Tars Tarkas the Thark. He did not see me land but just then the three opposing warriors—I recognized them as Warhoons—charged simultaneously. The mighty fellow made quick work of one of them, but in stepping back for another thrust, he fell over a dead body and was down and at the mercy of his foes. Quick as lightning they were on him, and Tars Tarkas would have been gathered to his fathers in short order had I not sprung in front of him and engaged his adversaries. I had accounted for one of them when the mighty Thark regained his feet and quickly dispatched the other.

He gave me one look, and a slight smile touched his grim lips as, touching my shoulder, he said, "I would scarcely recognize you, John Carter, but there is no other mortal on Barsoom who would have done that for me. I think I have now learned that there is such a thing as friendship."

He said no more, nor was there opportunity, for the Warhoons were closing in on us, and together we fought, side by side, during all that long, hot afternoon, until the tide of battle turned and the remnant of the fierce Warhoon horde fell back to their thoats and fled into the gathering darkness. Ten thousand men had been engaged in that titanic struggle, and on the field of battle lay three thousand dead.

On our return to the city after the battle, we went directly to Tars Tarkas's quarters, where I was left alone while the chieftain attended the post-engagement council meeting. As I sat awaiting his return, I heard something move in an adjoining apartment. As I glanced up, I was attacked by a huge creature that threw me onto a pile of silks and furs. It was Woola—faithful, loving Woola! He had found his way back to Thark and, as Tars Tarkas later told me, had gone immediately to my former quarters where he had taken up his pathetic and seemingly hopeless watch for my return.

"Tal Hajus knows that you are here," said Tars Tarkas, on his return from the jeddak's quarters. "Sarkoja saw you as we were returning. Tal Hajus has ordered me to bring you to him tonight. I have ten thoats, John Carter; you may take your choice from among them, and I will accompany you to the nearest waterway that leads to Helium. Tars Tarkas may be a cruel green warrior, but he can be a friend as well. Come, we must start."

"And when you return, Tars Tarkas?"

"I will face the wild calots or worse, unless I get the chance to battle with Tal Hajus! That is what I have so long awaited."

"We will stay, Tars Tarkas, and see Tal Hajus tonight. You shall not sacrifice yourself, and it may be that tonight you get your chance at him."

He objected strenuously, saying that Tal Hajus often flew into wild fits of passion at the mere thought of the blow I had dealt him, and that if he ever laid his hands on me I would be subjected to the most horrible tortures.

I then told Tars Tarkas the story Sola had whispered that long ago night. He said little, but the great muscles of his face worked in passion and agony at the recollection of the horrors heaped on the only thing he had ever loved in all his cold, cruel, terrible existence.

He was no longer reluctant about going to see Tal Hajus, only saying that he would like to speak to Sarkoja first. At his request I accompanied him to her quarters, and the look of venomous hatred she cast at me was almost adequate compensation for any future misfortunes this accidental return to Thark might bring me.

"Sarkoja," said Tars Tarkas, "forty years ago you were instrumental in bringing about the torture and death of a woman named Gozava. I have just discovered that the warrior who loved that woman has learned of your part in the transaction. He may not kill you, Sarkoja, for it is not our custom, but there is nothing to prevent him tying one end of a strap around your neck and the other end to a wild thoat, merely to test your fitness to survive and help perpetuate our race. Having heard that he will contact you tomorrow, I thought it only right to warn you, for I am a just man. The River Iss is but a short pilgrimage, Sarkoja. Come, John Carter."

The next morning Sarkoja was gone, and she was never seen again.

In silence we hastened to the jeddak's palace, where we were immediately admitted to his presence; in fact, he could scarcely wait to see me and was standing up on his platform glowering at the entrance as I came in. "Strap him to that pillar!" he shrieked. "We shall see who dares strike the mighty Tal Hajus! Heat the irons; with my own hands I shall burn the eyes from his head so he will not pollute my person with his vile gaze!"

"Chieftains of Thark!" I shouted, turning to the assembled council and ignoring Tal Hajus, "I have been a chief among you, and today I have fought for Thark alongside her greatest warrior! You at least owe me a hearing. I have won that much today. You claim to be a just people . . . "

"Silence!" roared Tal Hajus. "Gag the creature and bind him as I command!"

"Justice, Tal Hajus!" exclaimed Lorquas Ptomel. "Who are you to set aside the customs of ages among the Tharks?"

"Yes, justice!" echoed a dozen voices, and so while Tal Hajus fumed and frothed, I continued:

"You are a courageous people and you love

bravery, but where was your mighty jeddak during the fighting today? I did not see him in the thick of battle; he was not there! He torments defenseless women and little children in his lair, but how recently has one of you seen him fight with men? Why even I, a midget beside him, felled him with a single blow of my fist. Is this the kind of warrior fit to be a Thark's jeddak? There stands beside me now a great Thark, a mighty warrior and a noble man! Chieftains! How does this sound, Tars Tarkas, Jeddak of Thark?"

A roar of deep-toned applause greeted this suggestion.

"It but remains for this council to command, and Tal Hajus must prove his fitness to rule. If he was a brave man he would invite Tars Tarkas to combat, but Tal Hajus is afraid. Tal Hajus, your jeddak, is a coward! With my bare hands I could kill him, and he knows it."

After I ceased there was tense silence, as all eyes were riveted upon Tal Hajus. He did not speak or move, but the blotchy green of his countenance turned livid, and the froth froze on his lips.

"Tal Hajus," said Lorquas Ptomel in a cold, hard voice, "never have I seen a jeddak of the Tharks so humiliated. There could be but one answer to this arraignment. We await it." And still Tal Hajus stood as though petrified.

"Chieftains," continued Lorquas Ptomel,

"shall the Jeddak, Tal Hajus, prove his fitness to rule over Tars Tarkas?"

There were twenty chieftains around the rostrum, and twenty swords flashed high in assent. There was no alternative. That decree was final, and so Tal Hajus drew his sword and advanced to meet Tars Tarkas.

The combat was soon over, and with his foot on the neck of the dead monster, Tars Tarkas became jeddak among the Tharks. His first act was to make me a full-fledged chieftain with the rank I had won by my combats the first few weeks of my captivity among them. Seeing the favorable disposition of the warriors toward Tars Tarkas, as well as toward me, I grasped the opportunity to enlist them in my cause against Zodanga. I told Tars Tarkas the story of my adventures, and in a few words had explained to him the plan I had in mind.

He addressed the council and said, "John Carter has made a proposal which meets with my sanction. I shall put it to you briefly. Dejah Thoris, Princess of Helium, who was once our prisoner, is now held prisoner by the Jeddak of Zodanga. She must wed the jeddak's son to save her country from devastation at the hands of the Zodangan forces.

"John Carter suggests that we attack Zodanga, rescue the princess, and return her to Helium. The loot of Zodanga would be magnificent. In addition, I have often thought that if we had an alliance with the people of Helium we could obtain sufficient food and other resources to permit us to increase the size and frequency of our hatchings, and thus become supreme among the green men of all Barsoom! What say you?"

It was a chance to fight and an opportunity to loot, and they rose to the bait as a speckled trout to a fly. For Tharks they were wildly enthusiastic, and before another half hour had passed twenty mounted messengers were speeding off to call the hordes together for the expedition. In three days we were on the march toward Zodanga, one hundred thousand strong. In addition to the Tharks, Tars Tarkas had been able to enlist the services of several smaller hordes on the promise of plunder from the sack of the city.

At the head of the column I rode beside the great Thark while at my mount's heels trotted my beloved Woola. On the march, Tars Tarkas, through his remarkable statesmanship, enlisted fifty thousand more warriors from various hordes. Ten days after we set out we halted at midnight outside the great walled city of Zodanga, one hundred and fifty thousand strong.

The fighting strength and efficiency of this horde of ferocious green monsters was equivalent to ten times their number of red men. Never in the history of Barsoom had such a force of green warriors marched into battle together. It was a monstrous task to keep even a semblance of harmony among them, and it was a marvel to me that he got them to the city without a battle among themselves. But as we neared Zodanga their personal quarrels were diminished by their greater hatred for the red men, and especially for the Zodangans, who had for years waged a ruthless campaign of extermination against the green men, directing special attention toward tearing up their incubators.

Now that we were at Zodanga, the task of obtaining entry to the city was assigned to me. I directed Tars Tarkas to hold his forces in two divisions out of sight of the city, with each division opposite a large gateway. I took twenty dismounted warriors and approached one of the small gates that pierced the walls at short intervals. These gates have no regular guard, but are covered by sentries, who patrol the avenue that encircles the city just inside the walls.

The walls of Zodanga are seventy-five feet in height and fifty feet thick. The task of entering the city seemed impossible to my escort of green warriors. The fellows who had been detailed to accompany me were from one of the smaller hordes, and therefore did not know about my bottomless bag of tricks.

We snuck up to the wall and I placed three warriors with their faces to the wall and arms locked together. I then commanded two more to climb up onto their shoulders, and ordered a sixth to climb up on the shoulders of the upper two. The head of the topmost warrior towered almost forty feet from the ground.

In this way, with four more warriors, I built a series of steps from the ground to within a few feet of the top of the wall. Then, starting from a short distance away, I ran up from one warrior to the next, and with a final bound from the broad shoulders of the highest man I clutched the top of the wall and quietly pulled myself up. I then dragged a long length of leather up after me. Passing one end down to the topmost warrior I lowered the other end cautiously over the opposite side of the wall to the avenue below. No one was in sight, so lowering myself to the end of this leather strap, I dropped the remaining distance to the pavement below and then watched as the strap was drawn back over the top of the wall.

I had learned from Kantos Kan the secret of opening this city's gates, and in another moment my twenty green fighting men stood inside the doomed city of Zodanga. I found to my delight that I had entered at the lower boundary of the enormous palace grounds. The palace showed a blaze of glorious light, and at that moment I decided to lead a detachment of warriors directly to the palace itself, while the balance of the great horde was attacking the barracks of the troops.

I dispatched one of my men to Tars Tarkas with word of my intentions and a request for a detail of fifty Tharks. I ordered ten warriors to capture and open one of the great gates to the outside further down the wall while with the nine remaining I would attack the other. We were to do our work quietly, no shots were to be fired and no general advance made until I had reached the palace with my new detachment of fifty Tharks. Our plans worked to perfection. The two sentries we met were dispatched to their fathers upon the banks of the River Iss, and the guards at both large gates followed them in silence.

The Looting of Zodanga

As the gate where I stood swung open, my fifty Tharks, headed by Tars Tarkas himself, rode in on their mighty thoats. I led them to the palace walls, which I negotiated easily without assistance. Once I jumped over the wall, however, opening the palace gate gave me considerable trouble, but I finally got it to swing open on its huge hinges, and soon my fierce companions were riding across the gardens of the Jeddak of Zodanga.

As we approached the palace I could see through the windows into the brilliantly illuminated audience chamber. The immense hall was crowded with nobles and their women, as though some important function was in progress. There was not a guard in sight outside the palace, due, I presume, to the fact that the city and palace walls were considered impregnable, and so I came close and peered inside.

At one end of the chamber, on a massive golden throne encrusted with diamonds, sat Than Kosis. As I looked, I saw a procession advance from the far end of the hall toward the foot of the throne.

First marched four officers of the jeddak's Guard bearing a huge platter on which was placed a heavy golden chain with a collar and padlock at each end. Directly behind these officers came four others carrying the magnificent ornaments of the reigning house of Zodanga.

At the foot of the throne these two parties separated and halted, facing each other on opposite sides of the aisle. Then came more dignitaries, and officers of the palace and army, and finally two figures entirely muffled in scarlet silk, so that no feature of either could be seen. These two stopped at the foot of the throne facing Than Kosis. When the balance of the procession had entered and assumed their stations, Than Kosis addressed the couple standing before him. I could not hear his words, but then two officers advanced and removed the scarlet robe from one of the figures, and I saw that Kantos Kan had failed in his mission, for it was Sab Than, Prince of Zodanga. Than Kosis placed one of the collars of gold around his son's neck, securing it with a padlock. He then turned to the other figure, from which the officers now removed the enshrouding silks, revealing Dejah Thoris, Princess of Helium.

The object of the ceremony was clear to me—in another moment Dejah Thoris would be joined forever to the Prince of Zodanga! It was an impressive and beautiful ceremony, I presume, but to me it seemed the most fiendish sight I had ever witnessed. As the ornaments were adjusted on her beautiful figure and her collar of gold swung open in the hands of Than Kosis, I raised my sword above my head, shattered the window with the hilt, and jumped into the midst of the astonished assemblage! With a bound I was on the steps of the platform beside Than Kosis and brought my sword down upon the golden chain that would have bound Dejah Thoris to another man, severing it completely.

In an instant all was confusion! A thousand drawn swords menaced me from every quarter, and Sab Than advanced toward me with a jeweled dagger he had drawn from his nuptial ornaments. I could have killed him as easily as I might a fly, but the age-old custom of Barsoom stayed my hand. Grasping his wrist as the dagger flew toward my heart I held him away and, with my sword, pointed to the far end of the hall.

"Zodanga has fallen," I cried. "Look!"

All eyes turned, and there, forging through the portals of the entranceway rode Tars Tarkas and his fifty warriors on their immense wild thoats. A cry of alarm broke from the assemblage, but no word of fear, and in a moment the soldiers and nobles of Zodanga were hurling themselves on the advancing Tharks.

Throwing Sab Than headlong from the platform, I drew Dejah Thoris to my side. Behind the throne was a narrow doorway where Than Kosis now stood facing me with drawn sword. In an instant we were engaged, and I found no easy antagonist.

As we circled on the broad platform, I saw Sab Than rushing up the steps to aid his father, but as he raised his hand to strike, Dejah Thoris dashed in front of him. My sword soon found the spot that made Sab Than the Jeddak of Zodanga! As his father rolled dead on the floor the new jeddak tore himself free from Dejah Thoris's grasp, and again we faced each other. He was soon joined by a quartet of officers, and with my back against a golden throne, I fought once again for Dejah Thoris. I was hard pressed to defend myself and yet not strike down Sab Than and with him, my last chance to win the woman I loved. My blade was swinging with the speed of lightning as I sought to parry the thrusts and cuts of my opponents. Two I had disarmed, and one was down, when several more rushed to the aid of their new ruler and to avenge the death of the old.

As they advanced there were cries of "The

woman! The woman! Strike her down! It is her plot. Kill her! Kill her!"

Calling to Dejah Thoris to get behind me, I worked my way toward the little doorway in back of the throne, but the officers realized my intentions, and three of them ran in behind me and blocked me from a position where I could have defended Dejah Thoris.

The Tharks were having their hands full in the center of the room, and I began to realize that nothing short of a miracle could save us up on this platform. Then I saw Tars Tarkas surging through the crowd that swarmed around him! With one swing of his mighty sword, he laid a dozen corpses at his feet, and so he cut a pathway before him until in another moment he stood on the platform beside me, dealing death and destruction right and left.

The bravery of the Zodangans was awe-inspiring—not one attempted to escape, and when the fighting ceased it was because—other than Dejah Thoris and myself—only Tharks remained alive in the great hall. Sab Than lay dead beside his father, and the flower of Zodangan nobility and chivalry covered the floor in bloody shambles.

After the battle was over my first thought was for Kantos Kan. I took a dozen warriors and ran down to the dungeons beneath the palace. The jailers had all left to join the fighters in the throne room, so we searched the prison without opposition. I called Kantos Kan's name aloud in each new corridor and compartment and finally was rewarded by hearing a faint response. Guided by the sound, we soon found him and he was overjoyed at seeing me. He told me that the air patrol had captured him before he reached the high tower of the palace, so that he had not even seen Sab Than. Soon we had Kantos Kan with us in the throne room.

The sounds of heavy fighting, mingled with shouts and cries, came to us from the city's streets, and Tars Tarkas left to direct the action. Kantos Kan accompanied him to act as guide while the green warriors commenced a search of the palace for other Zodangans and, of course, for loot. At last, Dejah Thoris and I were left alone.

She had sunk into the golden throne, and as I turned to her she greeted me with a wan smile. "Was there ever such a man!" she exclaimed. "I know that Barsoom has never before seen your like. Can it be that all Earthmen are like you? Alone, a stranger, hunted, threatened, persecuted, you have done in a few short months what in all the past ages of Barsoom no man has ever done: joined together the wild hordes of the sea bottoms and brought them to fight as allies of a red Martian people!"

"The answer is easy, Dejah Thoris," I replied smiling. "It was not John Carter who did it, it was my love, my love for you, a power that could work even greater miracles than what you have seen today."

A pretty flush spread over her face and she answered, "You may say that now, John Carter, and I may listen, for I am free."

"I have more to say before it is again too late," I spoke solemnly. "I have done many strange things in my life, many things that wiser men would not have dared, but never in my wildest dreams have I thought of winning a princess such as you for myself—for never had I dreamed that in all the universe there lived such a woman as the Princess of Helium. That you are a future queen does not intimidate me, but that you are you is enough to make me doubt my sanity as I ask you, my princess, to be mine."

"He does not need to be worried who so well knows the answer to his plea before the plea was made," she replied, rising and placing her hands on my shoulders, and so I took her in my arms and kissed her.

And thus, in the midst of a city of wild conflict, filled with the alarms of war; with death and destruction reaping their terrible harvest around her, did Dejah Thoris, Princess of Helium, true daughter of Mars, the God of War, promise herself in marriage to John Carter, Gentleman of Virginia.

Through Carnage to Joy

Sometime later Tars Tarkas and Kantos Kan returned to report that Zodanga had been completely reduced. Her forces were destroyed or captured, and no further resistance was expected. Several battleships had escaped, but there were thousands of war and merchant vessels under the guard of Thark warriors.

The lesser hordes had commenced looting and quarreling among themselves, so it was decided that we collect what warriors we could, man as many vessels as possible with Zodangan prisoners and make for Helium without further loss of time. Five hours later we sailed with a fleet of two hundred and fifty battleships, carrying nearly one hundred thousand green warriors. Our thoats followed in a fleet of transports a few miles to the rear. Behind us we left the stricken city in the fierce and brutal clutches of some forty thousand green warriors of the lesser hordes. They were looting, murdering, and fighting amongst themselves. In a hundred places they had put the city to the torch, and columns of dense smoke were rising above the city to blot out the horrid sights below from the eye of heaven.

In the middle of the afternoon we sighted the scarlet and yellow towers of Helium, and a short time later a great fleet of Zodangan battleships rose from the camps of the besiegers outside the city, and advanced to meet us. The banners of Helium had been strung from stem to stern of each of our mighty craft, but the Zodangans did not need this sign to realize that we were enemies, for our green Martian warriors had opened fire almost as the enemy left the ground. With their uncanny marksmanship they raked the oncoming fleet with volley after volley.

The twin cities of Helium, perceiving that we were friends, sent out hundreds of vessels to aid us, and then began the first real air battle I had ever witnessed. The vessels carrying our green warriors were kept circling above the contending fleets of Helium and Zodanga, since the ship's large weapons were useless in the hands of the Tharks who did not have the training to operate them. Their small-arm fire, however, was most effective, and the final outcome of the engagement was strongly influenced by their presence.

At first the two forces circled at the same altitude, pouring broadside after broadside into each other. Soon a large hole was torn in the hull of one of the immense battlecraft from the Zodangan camp. With a lurch she turned completely over, the little figures of her crew plunging, turning and twisting toward the ground a thousand feet below. With sickening velocity she tore after them, almost completely burying herself in the ancient sea bottom.

A wild cry arose from Helium's warships, and with redoubled ferocity they fell upon the Zodangan fleet. By a skilled maneuver, two of the Helium vessels gained position above their adversaries, from which they poured down a torrent of exploding bombs.

Then, one by one, the battleships of Helium succeeded in rising above the Zodangans, and in a short time a number of the enemy battleships were drifting wrecks. Several others attempted to escape, but they were soon surrounded by thousands of tiny individual fliers, and above each enemy battleship hung a monster battleship of Helium ready to drop boarding parties on their decks.

Within little more than an hour from the moment the Zodangan squadron had risen to meet us, the battle was over, and the remaining vessels of the conquered Zodangans were headed toward the cities of Helium with our warriors as prize crews.

nd in another moment they were being crushed
ike grain between two millstones. They fought
vell, but in vain.

The plain before the city became a veritable
shambles before the last Zodangan surrendered,
but finally the carnage ceased, the prisoners were
marched away, and we entered the city's gates, a
huge triumphal procession of conquering heroes.
The broad avenues were lined with women and
children, along with the few men who remained
within the city during the battle. We were greeted
with an endless round of applause and showered
with ornaments of gold, platinum, silver, and precious jewels. The city had gone mad with joy.

My fierce Tharks caused the wildest excitement and enthusiasm. Never before had an
armed body of green warriors entered the gates
of Helium, and that they came now as friends and
allies filled the red men with rejoicing. Even the
ferocious appearance of Woola failed to dampen
the adoration that the populace pressed on us. As
we approached the palace, a party of officers
requested that Tars Tarkas and his jeds dismount
and accompany them inside to receive expres-
sions of gratitude from Tardos Mors.

The royal party stood at the top of the steps
leading to the main portals of the palace, and as
we reached the lower steps one of their number
descended to meet us. He was an almost perfect
specimen of manhood: tall, straight as an arrow,

We now signaled the flagship of Helium's
navy for permission to approach, and when she
was within hailing distance I called out that we
had the Princess Dejah Thoris onboard, and that
we wished to transfer her to the flagship so that
she might be taken immediately to the city.

As the full impact of my announcement was
understood, a great cry arose from the decks of
the flagship, and a moment later the colors of the
Princess of Helium broke out from a hundred
points on her upper works. When the other vessels of the squadron caught the meaning of the
signals they took up the wild acclaim and also
unfurled her colors in the gleaming sunlight.

The flagship came toward us, and as she
swung gracefully around and touched our side, a
dozen officers jumped over onto our decks. As
their astonished gaze fell upon the hundreds of
green warriors, who now came out of the fighting shelters, they stopped in surprise, but at sight
of Kantos Kan, they rushed forward and crowded around him.

Dejah Thoris and I then advanced, and they
had no eyes for anyone other than her. She
received them gracefully, calling each by name,
for they were men high in the esteem and service
of her grandfather, and she knew them well.

"Lay your hands upon the shoulder of John
Carter," she said to them, turning toward me,
"the man to whom Helium owes her princess as

well as the victory today!"

They were very courteous to me and said many kind things, but what seemed to impress them most was that I had won the aid of the fierce Tharks in my campaign for the liberation of Dejah Thoris and the salvation of Helium.

"You owe your thanks more to another man," I said, "and here he is—meet one of Barsoom's greatest soldiers and statesmen, Tars Tarkas, Jeddak of Thark!"

With the same polished courtesy that had marked their manner toward me they extended their greetings to the great Thark, and to my surprise, he was not much behind them in ease of bearing or in courtly speech. Though not a talkative race, the Tharks are extremely formal, and their ways lend themselves amazingly well to dignified and courtly manners.

Dejah Thoris went aboard the flagship, and was disappointed that I would not follow, but, as I explained to her, the battle was only partly won; we still had the land forces of the besieging Zodangans to account for, and I would not leave Tars Tarkas until that had been accomplished.

The commander of the naval forces of Helium arranged to have their armies attack from the city at the same time as our attack from the plain, and so the vessels separated and Dejah Thoris was carried back to the court of her grandfather, Tardos Mors, Jeddak of Helium.

Our fleet of transports holding th warriors' thoats, was just a short dist where they had remained during the airs tle. As soon as the last thoat was unload Tarkas gave the command to advance, three parties we crept up on the Zodanga from the north, the south and the east. A mile from the main camp we encountere outposts and, as had been prearranged, ac this as the signal to charge. With wild, fer cries and amidst the nasty squealing of enraged thoats we engaged the Zodangans.

We did not catch them napping, but fo well-entrenched battle line confronting us. after time we were repulsed until, toward no began to fear for the result of the battle. Zodangans numbered nearly a million figh men, while pitted against them were less th hundred thousand green warriors. The fo from Helium had not arrived, nor had received any word from them.

Just at noon we heard heavy firing all alo the line between the Zodangans and the citi and we knew then that our much-needed rei forcements had arrived. Again Tars Tark ordered the charge, and once more the migh thoats bore their terrible riders against the defen sive fortifications of the enemy. At the sam moment the battle line of Helium surged ove the opposite defense-works of the Zodangans

superbly muscled and with the carriage and bearing of a ruler of men. I did not need to be told that he was Tardos Mors, Jeddak of Helium.

The first member of our party he met was Tars Tarkas and his words sealed the new friendship between the races, "That Tardos Mors, may meet the greatest living warrior of Barsoom is a priceless honor, but that he may lay his hand on the shoulder of a friend and ally is a far greater boon."

"Jeddak of Helium," answered Tars Tarkas, "it has remained for a man of another world to teach the green warriors of Barsoom the meaning of friendship; to him we owe the fact that the hordes of Thark can understand you and that they can appreciate and reciprocate the sentiments so graciously expressed."

Tardos Mors then greeted each of the green jeddaks and jeds, and to each spoke words of friendship and appreciation. As he approached me he laid both hands on my shoulders. "Welcome, my son," he said. "You are granted, gladly, and without one word of opposition, the most precious jewel in all Helium. I am sure that this is sufficient display of my esteem."

We were then presented to Mors Kajak, Jed of lesser Helium, and father of Dejah Thoris. He had followed close behind Tardos Mors and seemed even more affected by the meeting than had his father. He tried a dozen times to express his gratitude to me, but his voice choked with emotion and he could not speak, and yet he had a fighter's reputation for ferocity and fearlessness that was remarkable even on warlike Barsoom. He worshiped his daughter, and could not think of what she had escaped without deep emotion.

CHAPTER 27

From Joy to Death

For ten days the hordes of Thark and their wild allies were feasted and entertained, and then, loaded with costly presents and escorted by ten thousand soldiers of Helium commanded by Mors Kajak, they started on the return journey to their own lands. The Jed of lesser Helium, with a small party of nobles, accompanied them all the way to Thark to cement more closely the new bonds of peace and friendship. Sola also accompanied Tars Tarkas, her father, who before all his chieftains had acknowledged her as his daughter.

Three weeks later, Mors Kajak and his officers, accompanied by Tars Tarkas and Sola, returned. A battleship had been dispatched to Thark to fetch them in time for the ceremony that made Dejah Thoris and John Carter one.

For nine years I served in the councils and fought in the armies of Helium as a prince of the house of Tardos Mors. The people seemed never to tire of heaping honors on me; not a day passed without them showing some new proof of their love for my princess.

In a golden incubator on the roof of our palace lay a snow-white egg. For nearly five years soldiers of the jeddak's Guard had protected it, and every day when I was in the city, Dejah Thoris and I stood hand in hand before our little shrine planning for the future. Vivid in my memory is the picture of our last night as we sat there talking of the strange romance that had joined our lives together and of this wonder that was coming to add to our happiness and fulfill our hopes.

The next day we saw in the distance the bright-white light of an approaching airship. Like a bolt of lightning it raced toward Helium until its very speed warned of the unusual. Flashing emergency signals, it circled impatiently awaiting the patrol boat that would escort it to the palace docks. Minutes after it touched ground a messenger called me to the council chamber where I found Tardos Mors, pacing back and forth in front of his advisors. He turned toward me and said, "This morning word reached the several governments of Barsoom that the keeper of the atmosphere plant had made no wireless report for two days and all attempts to communicate with him have failed.

"We have been asked to find the assistant

keeper and convey him to the plant. All day a thousand cruisers have been searching for him. Word was just received that his dead body was found in the pits beneath his house.

"I do not need to tell you what this means to Barsoom. It would take months to penetrate those mighty walls, in fact the work has already commenced. There would be little to fear if the engine of the pumping plant were operating as it should, but the worst, we fear, has happened. The instruments show a rapidly decreasing air pressure on all parts of Barsoom—the pump engine has stopped."

"Gentlemen," he concluded, "we have at best three days to live."

There was absolute silence for several minutes, and then a young noble arose, and with his drawn sword held high above his head addressed Tardos Mors. "The men of Helium have always shown Barsoom how a nation of red men should live, now is our opportunity to show them how they should die. Let us go about our duties as though a thousand useful years still lay before us."

The chamber rang with applause and we went our ways with smiles on our faces and sorrow gnawing at our hearts—there was nothing better to do than to allay the fears of the people by our example.

When I returned to our palace I found that the rumor already had reached Dejah Thoris, so I told her all that I had heard. "We have been very happy, John Carter," she said, "and I hope whatever fate overtakes us permits us to die together."

The next two days brought no noticeable change in the supply of air, but on the morning of the third day breathing became difficult at the higher altitudes of the rooftops. The avenues and plazas of Helium were filled with people. All business had ceased. For the most part the people looked bravely into the face of their unalterable doom. Here and there, however, men and women gave way to quiet grief. Toward the middle of the day many of the weaker started to succumb and within an hour the people of Barsoom were sinking by thousands into the unconsciousness that precedes death by suffocation.

Dejah Thoris and I, with the other members of the royal family, had joined together in a sunken garden within an inner courtyard of the jeddak's palace. Even Woola seemed to feel the weight of the impending calamity, for he pressed close to Dejah Thoris and me, whining pitifully. The little incubator had been brought from the roof of our palace and now my wife and princess sat gazing upon the unborn life that she would never know.

Tardos Mors arose, saying, "Let us bid each other farewell. The days of the greatness of Barsoom are over. Tomorrow's sun will look down upon a dead world. It is the end."

He stooped and kissed the women of his family, and laid his strong hand upon the shoulders of the men. As I turned sadly from him my eyes fell on Dejah Thoris. Her head was drooping and to all appearances she was lifeless. With a cry I sprang to her and held her in my arms.

Her eyes opened and looked into mine. "Kiss me, John Carter," she murmured. "I love you! I love you! It is cruel that we must be torn apart when we were just starting our life of love and happiness."

As I pressed her sweet lips to mine the old feeling of unconquerable power and authority rose in me. The fighting blood of Virginia sprang to life in my veins. "It shall not be, my princess!" I cried. "There must be some way, and John Carter, who has fought his way through a strange world for love of you, will find it!"

And with my words there crept above the threshold of my conscious mind a series of nine long forgotten sounds. Like a flash of lightning in the darkness their importance dawned on me— the key to the great doors of the atmosphere plant! Turning suddenly toward Tardos Mors as I still clasped my dying love in my arms, I exclaimed, "A flier, Jeddak! Quick! Order your swiftest flier here at once! I can save Barsoom!"

He did not wait to question, but in an instant a guard was racing to the nearest dock and though the air was thin and almost gone at the rooftop, they managed to launch the fastest one-man, air scout machine that the skill of Barsoom had ever produced.

Kissing Dejah Thoris a dozen times and commanding Woola, who would have followed me, to remain and guard her, I bounded with my old agility and strength to the flying machine, and in another moment I was headed out with all the hopes of Barsoom. I had to fly low to get sufficient air to breathe, but I took a straight course across an old sea bottom flying only a few feet above the ground.

I traveled with terrific speed on my race with death. The face of Dejah Thoris hung in front of me. As I turned for a last look as I left the palace garden I had seen her stagger and sink to the ground beside the little incubator. I knew that she had dropped into the coma that would end in death. So, throwing caution to the winds, I flung everything overboard but the engine and compass, and lying on my belly with one hand on the steering wheel and the other pushing the speed lever to its last notch, I split the thin air of dying Mars with the speed of a meteor.

An hour before dark the great walls of the atmosphere plant loomed before me, and I landed in front of the small door that was withholding the spark of life from the inhabitants of an entire planet. Beside the door a large crew of men had been laboring to pierce the wall, but they had scarcely scratched the flint-like surface, and now most of them lay in the last sleep from which not even air would awaken them. There were a few men still conscious, and to one of these I asked, "If I can open this door is there a man who can start the engines?"

"I can," he replied, "if you open it quickly. I can last but a few more moments. But it is useless, no one knows the secret of this awful lock. For three days men crazed with fear have surged around this door and failed in their attempts to solve its mystery."

I had no time to talk, I was becoming very weak and it was with difficulty that I controlled my mind at all. But, with a final effort, as I sank weakly to my knees I hurled the nine thought waves at that awful thing in front of me. The Martian had crawled to my side, and with staring eyes fixed on the single panel before us, we waited in the silence of death.

Slowly the door receded before us. I attempted to rise and follow the pathway but I was too weak. "Go!" I cried to my companion, "and if you reach the pump room start up all the pumps. It is the only chance Barsoom has to exist tomorrow!"

From where I lay I opened the second door, and then the third, and as I saw the hope of Barsoom crawling weakly on hands and knees through the last doorway I sank unconscious to the ground.

At the Arizona Cave

It was dark when I opened my eyes. Strange, stiff garments were on my body; garments that cracked and turned to dust as I rose to a sitting position. I felt myself over from head to foot and found I was clothed, though when I fell unconscious at the little doorway of the atmosphere plant I had been naked. Above me was a small patch of moonlit sky that showed through a ragged crack in the rocks.

As my hands passed over my body I found a pocket with a small parcel of matches. I struck one of these and its dim flame lit up what appeared to be a huge cave. In the back I discovered a strange, still figure huddled over a tiny bench. As I approached it I saw that it was the mummified remains of a little old woman with long gray hair. She was leaning over a round copper vessel containing a small quantity of greenish powder.

Behind her, hung from the roof and stretching across the cave on rawhide thongs, was a row of human skeletons. Another thong stretched from them to the dead hand of the little old woman; as I touched it the skeletons moved with a noise like the rustling of dry leaves. It was a most grotesque and horrid scene and I ran out into the fresh air, glad to escape. The sight that met my eyes as I left the cave filled me with both wonder and horror.

A new heaven and a new landscape met my gaze. The silvered mountains in the distance, the stationary moon hanging in the sky, the cactus-filled valley below—were not Mars! I could scarcely believe my eyes, but the truth slowly dawned on me—I was looking out at Arizona from the same ledge where ten years before I had gazed with longing upon the red planet.

Burying my head in my arms I turned and walked down the trail from the cave. Above me shone Mars, holding her awful secret, forty-eight million miles away. Did the Martian at the atmosphere factory get to the pump room? Did the life giving air reach the people of that distant planet in time to save them? Was my Dejah Thoris alive, or did her beautiful body lie cold in death beside the tiny golden incubator in the palace of Tardos Mors, the Jeddak of Helium?

For ten years I have prayed for an answer to my questions. For ten years I have waited to be taken back to the world of my lost love. I would rather lie dead beside her on Mars than live on Earth all those millions of terrible miles away.

I returned to the gold mine and found it untouched. It has made me fabulously wealthy—but what do I care for wealth? As I sit here tonight in my study overlooking the Hudson River, just twenty years have passed since I first opened my eyes on Mars. I can see her shining in the sky through the window by my desk, and tonight she seems to be calling to me again.

I think I can see, across that awful abyss of space, a beautiful black-haired woman standing in the garden of a palace, and at her side is a little boy who puts his arm around her as she points into the sky toward the planet Earth, while at their feet is a huge and hideous creature with a heart of gold. I believe they are waiting for me, and something tells me that I will soon know.

Afterword

"I am a hundred years old, maybe more. . . . I can only describe in the words of an ordinary soldier of fortune the strange events that happened to me during the ten years that my dead body lay in an Arizona cave."

You have to hand it to Edgar Rice Burroughs —he knew how to grab a reader's attention. By the time we finish the second paragraph of *A Princess of Mars*, we are intrigued, to say the least. Our storyteller is at least a hundred years old, and his dead body lay in a cave for ten years? What in the world is going on?

Of course, as we'll soon learn (and may have suspected from the book's title), this story isn't taking place in *our* world. Instead, our hero, Captain John Carter of Virginia, is somehow magically transported to the planet of Mars.

And what a planet it is! Unlike modern writers, Burroughs (who published this work in 1912) was not burdened with a reading public who knew much about the red planet. Since the first spacecraft visited Mars in 1965, we Earthlings have been on the receiving end of a steady stream of information, and even photographs, of the planet. While there is still much we don't know about Mars, we do know a lot more than Burroughs did. For instance, the average temperature on Mars is 67 degrees below zero. Very strong winds, enormous dust storms, and even fierce tornadoes sometimes sweep the planet. No oxygen is present. There are polar ice caps, but no liquid water. In short, it doesn't sound like a place where beautiful princesses, 12-foot tall green men, white apes, doglike calots, or milk-producing plants would flourish.

But fortunately, Burroughs didn't have to deal with any of those pesky facts. Although he lived before the age of space exploration, he was writing at a time when technology was accomplishing incredible things. The fabulous (but doomed) Titanic had just been constructed; the Model T was on the road; Thomas Edison had created the first motion picture. Albert Einstein had published his theory of relativity. The word "vitamin" had just been coined to describe new medical discoveries. Change and exploration and discovery were in the air. Curiosity was running high about what was "out there"—in the depths of the oceans, in the heart of the jungles, even on other planets. Readers were open-minded, ready and eager to imagine fantastic new worlds—the kind that Burroughs was a master at creating.

Consider what Burroughs actually accomplishes in *A Princess of Mars*. He not only tells an exciting story, but he invents a whole world in which that story can take place. Sure, he calls that world "Mars," but as we've seen, the Mars that Dejah Thoris, Tars Tarkas, Sola and the rest called home bears almost no resemblance to the real red planet. Burroughs just borrowed a convenient name for his creation, which its inhabitants call Barsoom.

And inventing a new world, as Burroughs has done here, presents special challenges to a writer. If he were setting his story in Chicago, for instance, he could expect readers to picture the setting more or less accurately. Even if they had never visited Chicago, they would probably have a general idea what a large city in the American Midwest looked like. But Barsoom existed only in Burrough's imagination. He couldn't expect the reader to picture *anything*, unless he described it to them. Therefore, he has to describe absolutely everything: the plant and animal life, the appearance of the skies, the geography, the weather, the buildings, the streets, the vehicles, and so on. In addition, he must explain the civilizations living on Barsoom: the brutal Tharks, the advanced people of Helium, the gorilla-like white apes.

It would be more convenient for Burroughs if he could just devote the first couple of chapters to telling us every detail about Barsoom, but he's too skillful a writer for that. He knows that he has to insert those details naturally while he keeps his story moving quickly along. Otherwise his readers will lose interest. And one thing Edgar Rice Burroughs *never* allows is for his readers to lose interest. From his opening words about a 100-year-old man who had been dead for ten years, but who is now somehow telling the tale, it's apparent that this is a master storyteller. After those opening lines, the action begins with a bang and never lets up for more than a page or two. There is the discovery of a gold mine, then an ambush and death; the stumbling into an enchanted cave; the transport to Mars; death-defying battles; the rescue of a beautiful maiden; the single-handed taming of fearsome Martian beasts; the defeat of the local warriors—and by then we're still only in the early chapters!

Because of his Mars series (there were eventually eleven books about John Carter and his Martian adventures) Burroughs is sometimes referred to as the "grandfather of science fiction." But the truth is, *A Princess of Mars* and the books that followed it don't really fall in the "science fiction" category. Science fiction is based in science, and as we've learned, Burroughs's Mars books have little if any science to back them up. They're better described as fantasy, or even romantic fiction that just happens to take place on another planet. Whatever you call them, they've been providing readers with a lot of fun and thrills for nearly one hundred years.